Dear Reader,

I'm sorry to say that the book you are holding in your hands is extremely unpleasant. It tells an unhappy tale about three very unlucky children. Even though they are charming and clever, the Baudelaire siblings lead lives filled with misery and woe. From the very first page of this book when the children are at the beach and receive terrible news, continuing on through the entire story, disaster lurks at their heels. One might say they are magnets for misfortune.

In this short book alone, the three youngsters encounter a greedy and repulsive villain, itchy clothing, a disastrous fire, a plot to steal their fortune, and cold porridge for breakfast.

It is my sad duty to write down these unpleasant tales, but there is nothing stopping you from putting this book down at once and reading something happy, if you prefer that sort of thing.

With all due respect,

Lemony Snicket

Lemony Snicket

BOOK THE FIRST

THE BAD BEGINNING

A SERIES OF UNFORTUNATE EVENTS

A Series of Unfortunate Events

BOOK THE FIRST

THE BAD BEGINNING

by

Lemony Snicket

Illustrated by
BRETT HELQUIST

EGMONT

First published in Great Britain 2001
by Egmont Books Limited
239 Kensington High Street
London W8 6SA

First published in the USA 1999
by HarperCollins Children's Books
Published by arrangement with
HarperCollins Children's Books
A division of HarperCollins Publishers, Inc.
1350 Avenue of the Americas
New York, New York, USA

This edition published 2003
by Egmont Books Limited

ISBN 1 4052 0725 6

10 8 6 4 2 1 3 5 7 9

A CIP catalogue record for this book is available from the British Library

Printed and bound in Italy

To Beatrice –
darling, dearest, dead.

CHAPTER
One

If you are interested in stories with happy end-
ings, you would be better off reading some other
book. In this book, not only is there no happy
ending, there is no happy beginning and very
few happy things in the middle. This is because
not very many happy things happened in the
lives of the three Baudelaire youngsters. Violet,
Klaus, and Sunny Baudelaire were intelligent
children, and they were charming, and resource-
ful, and had pleasant facial features, but they
were extremely unlucky, and most everything
that happened to them was rife with misfortune,
misery, and despair. I'm sorry to tell you this,
but that is how the story goes.

Their misfortune began one day at Briny Beach. The three Baudelaire children lived with their parents in an enormous mansion at the heart of a dirty and busy city, and occasionally their parents gave them permission to take a rickety trolley—the word "rickety," you probably know, here means "unsteady" or "likely to collapse"—alone to the seashore, where they would spend the day as a sort of vacation as long as they were home for dinner. This particular morning it was gray and cloudy, which didn't bother the Baudelaire youngsters one bit. When it was hot and sunny, Briny Beach was crowded with tourists and it was impossible to find a good place to lay one's blanket. On gray and cloudy days, the Baudelaires had the beach to themselves to do what they liked.

Violet Baudelaire, the eldest, liked to skip rocks. Like most fourteen-year-olds, she was right-handed, so the rocks skipped farther across the murky water when Violet used her right hand than when she used her left. As she skipped rocks, she was looking out at the horizon and thinking about an invention she wanted to build. Anyone who knew Violet well could tell she was thinking hard, because her long hair was tied up in a ribbon to keep it out of her eyes. Violet had a real knack for inventing and building strange devices, so her brain was often filled with images of pulleys, levers, and gears, and she never wanted to be distracted by something as trivial as her hair. This morning she was thinking about how to construct a device that could retrieve a rock after you had skipped it into the ocean.

Klaus Baudelaire, the middle child, and the only boy, liked to examine creatures in tidepools. Klaus was a little older than twelve and wore glasses, which made him look intelligent. He *was* intelligent. The Baudelaire parents had an enormous library in their mansion, a room filled with thousands of books on nearly every subject. Being only twelve, Klaus of course had not read all of the books in the Baudelaire library, but he had read a great many of them and had retained a lot of the information from his readings. He knew how to tell an alligator from a crocodile. He knew who killed Julius Caesar. And he knew much about the tiny, slimy animals found at Briny Beach, which he was examining now.

Sunny Baudelaire, the youngest, liked to bite things. She was an infant, and very small for her age, scarcely larger than a boot. What she lacked in size, however, she made up for with the size and sharpness of her four teeth. Sunny was at an age where one mostly speaks in a series of unintelligible shrieks. Except when she used the few actual words in her vocabulary, like "bottle," "mommy," and "bite," most people had trouble understanding what it was that Sunny was saying. For instance, this morning she was saying "Gack!" over and over, which probably meant, "Look at that mysterious figure emerging from the fog!"

Sure enough, in the distance along the misty

shore of Briny Beach there could be seen a tall
figure striding toward the Baudelaire children.
Sunny had already been staring and shrieking
at the figure for some time when Klaus looked
up from the spiny crab he was examining, and
saw it too. He reached over and touched Violet's
arm, bringing her out of her inventing thoughts.

"Look at that," Klaus said, and pointed
toward the figure. It was drawing closer, and the
children could see a few details. It was about
the size of an adult, except its head was tall, and
rather square.

"What do you think it is?" Violet asked.

"I don't know," Klaus said, squinting at it,
"but it seems to be moving right toward us."

"We're alone on the beach," Violet said, a
little nervously. "There's nobody else it could
be moving toward." She felt the slender, smooth
stone in her left hand, which she had been
about to try to skip as far as she could. She had
a sudden thought to throw it at the figure, because it seemed so frightening.

"It only seems scary," Klaus said, as if reading his sister's thoughts, "because of all the mist."

This was true. As the figure reached them, the children saw with relief that it was not anybody frightening at all, but somebody they knew: Mr. Poe. Mr. Poe was a friend of Mr. and Mrs. Baudelaire's whom the children had met many times at dinner parties. One of the things Violet, Klaus, and Sunny really liked about their parents was that they didn't send their children away when they had company over, but allowed them to join the adults at the dinner table and participate in the conversation as long as they helped clear the table. The children remembered Mr. Poe because he always had a cold and was constantly excusing himself from the table to have a fit of coughing in the next room.

Mr. Poe took off his top hat, which had made his head look large and square in the fog, and stood for a moment, coughing loudly into a white handkerchief. Violet and Klaus moved forward to shake his hand and say how do you do.

"How do you do?" said Violet.

"How do you do?" said Klaus.

"Odo yow!" said Sunny.

"Fine, thank you," said Mr. Poe, but he looked very sad. For a few seconds nobody said anything, and the children wondered what Mr. Poe was doing there at Briny Beach, when he should have been at the bank in the city, where he worked. He was not dressed for the beach.

"It's a nice day," Violet said finally, making conversation. Sunny made a noise that sounded like an angry bird, and Klaus picked her up and held her.

"Yes, it is a nice day," Mr. Poe said absently, staring out at the empty beach. "I'm afraid I have some very bad news for you children."

The three Baudelaire siblings looked at him. Violet, with some embarrassment, felt the stone in her left hand and was glad she had not thrown it at Mr. Poe.

"Your parents," Mr. Poe said, "have perished in a terrible fire."

The children didn't say anything.

"They perished," Mr. Poe said, "in a fire that destroyed the entire house. I'm very, very sorry to tell you this, my dears."

Violet took her eyes off Mr. Poe and stared out at the ocean. Mr. Poe had never called the Baudelaire children "my dears" before. She understood the words he was saying but thought he must be joking, playing a terrible joke on her and her brother and sister.

"'Perished,'" Mr. Poe said, "means 'killed.'"

"We *know* what the word 'perished' means," Klaus said, crossly. He did know what the word "perished" meant, but he was still having trouble understanding exactly what it was that Mr. Poe had said. It seemed to him that Mr. Poe must somehow have misspoken.

"The fire department arrived, of course," Mr. Poe said, "but they were too late. The entire house was engulfed in fire. It burned to the ground."

Klaus pictured all the books in the library, going up in flames. Now he'd never read all of them.

Mr. Poe coughed several times into his handkerchief before continuing. "I was sent to retrieve you here, and to take you to my home, where you'll stay for some time while we figure things out. I am the executor of your parents' estate. That means I will be handling their enormous fortune and figuring out where you children will go. When Violet comes of age, the fortune will be yours, but the bank will take charge of it until you are old enough."

Although he said he was the executor, Violet felt like Mr. Poe was the executioner. He had simply walked down the beach to them and changed their lives forever.

"Come with me," Mr. Poe said, and held out his hand. In order to take it, Violet had to drop the stone she was holding. Klaus took Violet's other hand, and Sunny took Klaus's other hand, and in that manner the three Baudelaire children—the Baudelaire orphans, now—were led away from the beach and from their previous lives.

CHAPTER
Two

It is useless for me to describe to you how terrible Violet, Klaus, and even Sunny felt in the time that followed. If you have ever lost someone very important to you, then you already know how it feels, and if you haven't, you cannot possibly imagine it. For the Baudelaire children, it was of course especially

terrible because they had lost both their parents
at the same time, and for several days they felt
so miserable they could scarcely get out of bed.
Klaus found he had little interest in books. The
gears in Violet's inventive brain seemed to stop.
And even Sunny, who of course was too young
to really understand what was going on, bit
things with less enthusiasm.

Of course, it didn't make things any easier
that they had lost their home as well, and all
their possessions. As I'm sure you know, to be
in one's own room, in one's own bed, can often
make a bleak situation a little better, but the
beds of the Baudelaire orphans had been re-
duced to charred rubble. Mr. Poe had taken
them to the remains of the Baudelaire mansion
to see if anything had been unharmed, and it
was terrible: Violet's microscope had fused together in the heat of the fire, Klaus's favorite
pen had turned to ash, and all of Sunny's
teething rings had melted. Here and there, the
children could see traces of the enormous home

they had loved: fragments of their grand piano, an elegant bottle in which Mr. Baudelaire kept brandy, the scorched cushion of the windowseat where their mother liked to sit and read.

Their home destroyed, the Baudelaires had to recuperate from their terrible loss in the Poe household, which was not at all agreeable. Mr. Poe was scarcely at home, because he was very busy attending to the Baudelaire affairs, and when he was home he was often coughing so much he could barely have a conversation. Mrs. Poe purchased clothing for the orphans that was in grotesque colors, and itched. And the two Poe children—Edgar and Albert—were loud and obnoxious boys with whom the Baudelaires had to share a tiny room that smelled of some sort of ghastly flower.

But even given the surroundings, the children had mixed feelings when, over a dull dinner of boiled chicken, boiled potatoes and blanched—the word "blanched" here means "boiled"—string beans, Mr. Poe announced that they were to leave his household the next morning.

"Good," said Albert, who had a piece of potato stuck between his teeth. "Now we can get our room back. I'm tired of sharing it. Violet and Klaus are always moping around, and are never any fun."

"And the baby bites," Edgar said, tossing a chicken bone to the floor as if he were an animal in a zoo and not the son of a well-respected member of the banking community.

"Where will we go?" Violet asked nervously.

Mr. Poe opened his mouth to say something, but erupted into a brief fit of coughing. "I have made arrangements," he said finally, "for you to be raised by a distant relative of yours who lives on the other side of town. His name is Count Olaf."

Violet, Klaus, and Sunny looked at one another, unsure of what to think. On one hand, they didn't want to live with the Poes any longer. On the other hand, they had never heard of Count Olaf and didn't know what he would be like.

"Your parents' will," Mr. Poe said, "instructs that you be raised in the most convenient way possible. Here in the city, you'll be used to your surroundings, and this Count Olaf is the only relative who lives within the urban limits."

Klaus thought this over for a minute as he swallowed a chewy bit of bean. "But our parents never mentioned Count Olaf to us. Just how is he related to us, exactly?"

Mr. Poe sighed and looked down at Sunny, who was biting a fork and listening closely. "He is either a third cousin four times removed, or a fourth cousin three times removed. He is not your closest relative on the family tree, but he is the closest geographically. That's why—"

"If he lives in the city," Violet said, "why didn't our parents ever invite him over?"

"Possibly because he was very busy," Mr. Poe

said. "He's an actor by trade, and often travels around the world with various theater companies."

"I thought he was a count," Klaus said.

"He is both a count and an actor," Mr. Poe said. "Now, I don't mean to cut short our dinner, but you children have to pack up your things, and I have to return to the bank to do some more work. Like your new legal guardian, I am very busy myself."

The three Baudelaire children had many more questions for Mr. Poe, but he had already stood up from the table, and with a slight wave of his hand departed from the room. They heard him coughing into his handkerchief and then the front door creaked shut as he left the house.

"Well," Mrs. Poe said, "you three had better start packing. Edgar, Albert, please help me clear the table."

The Baudelaire orphans went to the bedroom and glumly packed their few belongings. Klaus

looked distastefully at each ugly shirt Mrs. Poe
had bought for him as he folded them and put
them into a small suitcase. Violet looked around
the cramped, smelly room in which they had
been living. And Sunny crawled around solemnly
biting each of Edgar and Albert's shoes, leaving
small teeth marks in each one so she would not
be forgotten. From time to time, the Baudelaire
children looked at one another, but with their
future such a mystery they could think of nothing to say. At bedtime, they tossed and turned all
night, scarcely getting any sleep between the
loud snoring of Edgar and Albert and their own
worried thoughts. Finally, Mr. Poe knocked on
the door and stuck his head into the bedroom.

"Rise and shine, Baudelaires," he said. "It's
time for you to go to Count Olaf's."

Violet looked around the crowded bedroom,
and even though she didn't like it, she felt very
nervous about leaving. "Do we have to go right
this minute?" she asked.

Mr. Poe opened his mouth to speak, but had to cough a few times before he began. "Yes you do. I'm dropping you off on my way to the bank, so we need to leave as soon as possible. Please get out of bed and get dressed," he said briskly. The word "briskly" here means "quickly, so as to get the Baudelaire children to leave the house."

The Baudelaire children left the house. Mr. Poe's automobile rumbled along the cobblestone streets of the city toward the neighborhood where Count Olaf lived. They passed horse-drawn carriages and motorcycles along Doldrum Drive. They passed the Fickle Fountain, an elaborately carved monument that occasionally spat out water in which young children played. They passed an enormous pile of dirt where the Royal Gardens once stood. Before too long, Mr. Poe drove his car down a narrow alley lined with houses made of pale brick and stopped halfway down the block.

"Here we are," Mr. Poe said, in a voice

undoubtedly meant to be cheerful. "Your new home."

The Baudelaire children looked out and saw the prettiest house on the block. The bricks had been cleaned very well, and through the wide and open windows one could see an assortment of well-groomed plants. Standing in the doorway, with her hand on the shiny brass doorknob, was an older woman, smartly dressed, who was smiling at the children. In one hand she carried a flowerpot.

"Hello there!" she called out. "You must be the children Count Olaf is adopting."

Violet opened the door of the automobile and got out to shake the woman's hand. It felt firm and warm, and for the first time in a long while Violet felt as if her life and the lives of her siblings might turn out well after all. "Yes," she said. "Yes, we are. I am Violet Baudelaire, and this is my brother Klaus and my sister Sunny. And this is Mr. Poe, who has been arranging things for us since the death of our parents."

"Yes, I heard about the accident," the woman said, as everyone said how do you do. "I am Justice Strauss."

"That's an unusual first name," Klaus remarked.

"It is my title," she explained, "not my first name. I serve as a judge on the High Court."

"How fascinating," Violet said. "And are you married to Count Olaf?"

"Goodness me no," Justice Strauss said. "I don't actually know him that well. He is my next-door neighbor."

The children looked from the well-scrubbed house of Justice Strauss to the dilapidated one next door. The bricks were stained with soot and grime. There were only two small windows, which were closed with the shades drawn even though it was a nice day. Rising above the windows was a tall and dirty tower that tilted slightly to the left. The front door needed to be repainted, and carved in the middle of it was an image of an eye. The entire building sagged to the side, like a crooked tooth.

"Oh!" said Sunny, and everyone knew what she meant. She meant, "What a terrible place! I don't want to live there at all!"

"Well, it was nice to meet you," Violet said to Justice Strauss.

"Yes," said Justice Strauss, gesturing to her flowerpot. "Perhaps one day you could come over and help me with my gardening."

"That would be very pleasant," Violet said, very sadly. It would, of course, be very pleasant to help Justice Strauss with her gardening, but Violet could not help thinking that it would be far more pleasant to live in Justice Strauss's house, instead of Count Olaf's. What kind of a man, Violet wondered, would carve an image of an eye into his front door?

Mr. Poe tipped his hat to Justice Strauss, who smiled at the children and disappeared into her lovely house. Klaus stepped forward and knocked on Count Olaf's door, his knuckles rapping right in the middle of the carved eye. There was a pause, and then the door creaked open and the children saw Count Olaf for the first time.

"Hello hello hello," Count Olaf said in a wheezy whisper. He was very tall and very thin, dressed in a gray suit that had many dark stains on it. His face was unshaven, and rather than two eyebrows, like most human beings have, he had just one long one. His eyes were very, very shiny, which made him look both hungry and angry. "Hello, my children. Please step into your new home, and wipe your feet outside so no mud gets indoors."

As they stepped into the house, Mr. Poe behind them, the Baudelaire orphans realized what a ridiculous thing Count Olaf had just said. The room in which they found themselves was the dirtiest they had ever seen, and a little bit of mud from outdoors wouldn't have made a bit of difference. Even by the dim light of the one bare lightbulb that hung from the ceiling, the three children could see that everything in this room was filthy, from the stuffed head of a lion which was nailed to the wall to the bowl of apple cores which sat on a small wooden table. Klaus willed himself not to cry as he looked around.

"This room looks like it needs a little work," Mr. Poe said, peering around in the gloom.

"I realize that my humble home isn't as fancy as the Baudelaire mansion," Count Olaf said, "but perhaps with a bit of your money we could fix it up a little nicer."

Mr. Poe's eyes widened in surprise, and his coughs echoed in the dark room before he spoke. "The Baudelaire fortune," he said sternly, "will not be used for such matters. In fact, it will not be used at all, until Violet is of age."

Count Olaf turned to Mr. Poe with a glint in his eye like an angry dog. For a moment Violet thought he was going to strike Mr. Poe across the face. But then he swallowed—the children could see his Adam's apple bob in his skinny throat—and shrugged his patchy shoulders.

"All right then," he said. "It's the same to me. Thank you very much, Mr. Poe, for bringing them here. Children, I will now show you to your room."

"Good-bye, Violet, Klaus, and Sunny," Mr. Poe said, stepping back through the front door. "I hope you will be very happy here. I will continue to see you occasionally, and you can always contact me at the bank if you have any questions."

"But we don't even know where the bank is," Klaus said.

"I have a map of the city," Count Olaf said. "Good-bye, Mr. Poe."

He leaned forward to shut the door, and the Baudelaire orphans were too overcome with despair to get a last glimpse of Mr. Poe. They now wished they could all stay at the Poe household, even though it smelled. Rather than looking at the door, then, the orphans looked down, and saw that although Count Olaf was wearing shoes, he wasn't wearing any socks. They could see, in the space of pale skin between his tattered trouser cuff and his black shoe, that Count Olaf had an image of an eye tattooed on his ankle, matching the eye on his front door. They wondered how many other eyes were in Count Olaf's house, and whether, for the rest of their lives, they would always feel as though Count Olaf were watching them even when he wasn't nearby.

CHAPTER Three

I don't know if you've ever noticed this, but first impressions are often entirely wrong. You can look at a painting for the first time, for example, and not like it at all, but after looking at it a little longer you may find it very pleasing. The first time you try Gorgonzola cheese you may find it too strong, but when you are older you may want to eat nothing but Gorgonzola cheese. Klaus, when Sunny was born, did not like her at all, but by the time she was six weeks old the two of them were thick as thieves. Your initial opinion on just about anything may change over time.

I wish I could tell you that the Baudelaires' first impressions of Count Olaf and his house were incorrect, as first impressions so often are. But these impressions—that Count Olaf was a horrible person, and his house a depressing pigsty—were absolutely correct. During the first few days after the orphans' arrival at Count Olaf's, Violet, Klaus, and Sunny attempted to make themselves feel at home, but it was really no use. Even though Count Olaf's house was quite large, the three children were placed together in one filthy bedroom that had only one small bed in it. Violet and Klaus took turns sleeping in it, so that every other night one of them was in the bed and the other was sleeping on the hard wooden floor, and the bed's mattress was so lumpy it was difficult to say who was more uncomfortable. To make a bed for Sunny, Violet removed the dusty curtains from the curtain rod that hung over the bedroom's one window and bunched them together to form a sort of cushion, just big enough for her sister. However, without curtains over the cracked glass, the sun streamed through the window every morning, so the children woke up early and sore each day. Instead of a closet, there was a large cardboard box that had once held a refrigerator and would now hold the three children's clothes, all piled in a heap. Instead of toys, books, or other things to amuse the youngsters, Count Olaf had provided a small pile of rocks. And the only decoration on the peeling walls was a large and ugly painting of an eye, matching the one on Count Olaf's ankle and all over the house.

But the children knew, as I'm sure you know, that the worst surroundings in the world can be tolerated if the people in them are interesting and kind. Count Olaf was neither interesting nor kind; he was demanding, short-tempered, and bad-smelling. The only good thing to be said for Count Olaf is that he wasn't around very often. When the children woke up and chose their clothing out of the refrigerator box, they would walk into the kitchen and find a list of instructions left for them by Count Olaf, who would often not appear until nighttime. Most of the day he spent out of the house, or up in the high tower, where the children were forbidden to go. The instructions he left for them were usually difficult chores, such as repainting the back porch or repairing the windows, and instead of a signature Count Olaf would draw an eye at the bottom of the note.

One morning his note read, "My theater troupe will be coming for dinner before tonight's performance. Have dinner ready for all ten of them by the time they arrive at seven o'clock. Buy the food, prepare it, set the table, serve dinner, clean up afterwards, and stay out of our way." Below that there was the usual eye, and underneath the note was a small sum of money for the groceries.

Violet and Klaus read the note as they ate their breakfast, which was a gray and lumpy oatmeal Count Olaf left for them each morning in a large pot on the stove. Then they looked at each other in dismay.

"None of us knows how to cook," Klaus said.

"That's true," Violet said. "I knew how to repair those windows, and how to clean the chimney, because those sorts of things interest me. But I don't know how to cook anything except toast."

"And sometimes you burn the toast," Klaus said, and they smiled. They were both remembering a time when the two of them got up early to make a special breakfast for their parents. Violet had burned the toast, and their parents, smelling smoke, had run downstairs to see what the matter was. When they saw Violet and Klaus, looking forlornly at pieces of pitch-black toast, they laughed and laughed, and then made pancakes for the whole family.

"I wish they were here," Violet said. She did

not have to explain she was talking about their parents. "They would never let us stay in this dreadful place."

"If they were here," Klaus said, his voice rising as he got more and more upset, "we would not be with Count Olaf in the first place. I *hate* it here, Violet! I *hate* this house! I *hate* our room! I *hate* having to do all these chores, and I *hate* Count Olaf!"

"I hate it too," Violet said, and Klaus looked at his older sister with relief. Sometimes, just saying that you hate something, and having someone agree with you, can make you feel better about a terrible situation. "I hate everything about our lives right now, Klaus," she said, "but we have to keep our chin up." This was an expression the children's father had used, and it meant "try to stay cheerful."

"You're right," Klaus said. "But it is very difficult to keep one's chin up when Count Olaf keeps shoving it down."

"Jook!" Sunny shrieked, banging on the table

with her oatmeal spoon. Violet and Klaus were jerked out of their conversation and looked once again at Count Olaf's note.

"Perhaps we could find a cookbook, and read about how to cook," Klaus said. "It shouldn't be that difficult to make a simple meal."

Violet and Klaus spent several minutes opening and shutting Count Olaf's kitchen cupboards, but there weren't any cookbooks to be found.

"I can't say I'm surprised," Violet said. "We haven't found any books in this house at all."

"I know, " Klaus said miserably. "I miss reading very much. We must go out and look for a library sometime soon."

"But not today," Violet said. "Today we have to cook for ten people."

At that moment there was a knock on the front door. Violet and Klaus looked at one another nervously.

"Who in the world would want to visit Count Olaf?" Violet wondered out loud.

"Maybe somebody wants to visit *us*," Klaus said, without much hope. In the time since the Baudelaire parents' death, most of the Baudelaire orphans' friends had fallen by the wayside, an expression which here means "they stopped calling, writing, and stopping by to see any of the Baudelaires, making them very lonely." You and I, of course, would never do this to any of our grieving acquaintances, but it is a sad truth in life that when someone has lost a loved one, friends sometimes avoid the person, just when the presence of friends is most needed.

Violet, Klaus, and Sunny walked slowly to the front door and peered through the peephole, which was in the shape of an eye. They were delighted to see Justice Strauss peering back at them, and opened the door.

"Justice Strauss!" Violet cried. "How lovely to see you." She was about to add, "Do come in," but then she realized that Justice Strauss would probably not want to venture into the dim and dirty room.

"Please forgive me for not stopping by sooner," Justice Strauss said, as the Baudelaires stood awkwardly in the doorway. "I wanted to see how you children were settling in, but I had a very difficult case in the High Court and it was taking up much of my time."

"What sort of case was it?" Klaus asked. Having been deprived of reading, he was hungry for new information.

"I can't really discuss it," Justice Strauss said, "because it's official business. But I can tell you it concerns a poisonous plant and illegal use of someone's credit card."

"Yeeka!" Sunny shrieked, which appeared to mean "How interesting!" although of course there is no way that Sunny could understand what was being said.

Justice Strauss looked down at Sunny and laughed. "Yeeka indeed," she said, and reached down to pat the child on the head. Sunny took Justice Strauss's hand and bit it, gently.

"That means she likes you," Violet explained.

"She bites very, very hard if she doesn't like you, or if you want to give her a bath."

"I see," Justice Strauss said. "Now then, how are you children getting on? Is there anything you desire?"

The children looked at one another, thinking of all the things they desired. Another bed, for example. A proper crib for Sunny. Curtains for the window in their room. A closet instead of a cardboard box. But what they desired most of all, of course, was not to be associated with Count Olaf in any way whatsoever. What they desired most was to be with their parents again, in their true home, but that, of course, was impossible. Violet, Klaus, and Sunny all looked down at the floor unhappily as they considered the question. Finally, Klaus spoke.

"Could we perhaps borrow a cookbook?" he said. "Count Olaf has instructed us to make dinner for his theater troupe tonight, and we can't find a cookbook in the house."

"Goodness," Justice Strauss said. "Cooking

dinner for an entire theater troupe seems like a lot to ask of children."

"Count Olaf gives us a lot of responsibility," Violet said. What she wanted to say was, "Count Olaf is an evil man," but she was well mannered.

"Well, why don't you come next door to my house," Justice Strauss said, "and find a cookbook that pleases you?"

The youngsters agreed, and followed Justice Strauss out the door and over to her well-kept house. She led them through an elegant hallway smelling of flowers into an enormous room, and when they saw what was inside, they nearly fainted from delight, Klaus especially.

The room was a library. Not a public library, but a private library; that is, a large collection of books belonging to Justice Strauss. There were shelves and shelves of them, on every wall from the floor to the ceiling, and separate shelves and shelves of them in the middle of the room. The only place there weren't books was in one corner, where there were some large, comfortable-looking chairs and a wooden table with lamps hanging over them, perfect for reading. Although it was not as big as their parents' library, it was as cozy, and the Baudelaire children were thrilled.

"My word!" Violet said. "This is a wonderful library!"

"Thank you very much," Justice Strauss said. "I've been collecting books for years, and I'm very proud of my collection. As long as you keep them in good condition, you are welcome to use any of my books, at any time. Now, the cookbooks are over here on the eastern wall. Shall we have a look at them?"

"Yes," Violet said, "and then, if you don't mind, I should love to look at any of your books concerning mechanical engineering. Inventing things is a great interest of mine."

"And I would like to look at books on wolves," Klaus said. "Recently I have been fascinated by the subject of wild animals of North America."

"Book!" Sunny shrieked, which meant "Please don't forget to pick out a picture book for me."

Justice Strauss smiled. "It is a pleasure to see young people interested in books," she said. "But first I think we'd better find a good recipe, don't you?"

The children agreed, and for thirty minutes or so they perused several cookbooks that Justice Strauss recommended. To tell you the truth, the three orphans were so excited to be out of Count Olaf's house, and in this pleasant library, that they were a little distracted and unable to concentrate on cooking. But finally Klaus found a dish that sounded delicious, and easy to make.

"Listen to this," he said. "'Puttanesca.' It's an Italian sauce for pasta. All we need to do is sauté olives, capers, anchovies, garlic, chopped parsley, and tomatoes together in a pot, and pre-pare spaghetti to go with it."

"That sounds easy," Violet agreed, and the

Baudelaire orphans looked at one another. Perhaps, with the kind Justice Strauss and her library right next door, the children could prepare pleasant lives for themselves as easily as making puttanesca sauce for Count Olaf.

CHAPTER

Four

The Baudelaire orphans copied the puttanesca
recipe from the cookbook onto a piece of scrap
paper, and Justice Strauss was
kind enough to escort them to
the market to buy the necessary ingredients. Count Olaf
had not left them very
much money, but the chil-
dren were able to buy
everything they needed.
From a street vendor,
they purchased olives
after tasting several

varieties and choosing their favorites. At a pasta store they selected interestingly shaped noodles and asked the woman running the store the proper amount for thirteen people—the ten people Count Olaf mentioned, and the three of them. Then, at the supermarket, they purchased garlic, which is a sharp-tasting bulbous plant; anchovies, which are small salty fish; capers, which are flower buds of a small shrub and taste marvelous; and tomatoes, which are actually fruits and not vegetables as most people believe. They thought it would be proper to serve dessert, and bought several envelopes of pudding mix. Perhaps, the orphans thought, if they made a delicious meal, Count Olaf might be a bit kinder to them.

"Thank you so much for helping us out today," Violet said, as she and her siblings walked home with Justice Strauss. "I don't know what we would have done without you."

"You seem like very intelligent people," Justice Strauss said. "I daresay you would have thought of something. But it continues to strike me as odd that Count Olaf has asked you to prepare such an enormous meal. Well, here we are. I must go inside and put my own groceries away. I hope you children will come over soon and borrow books from my library."

"Tomorrow?" Klaus said quickly. "Could we come over tomorrow?"

"I don't see why not," Justice Strauss said, smiling.

"I can't tell you how much we appreciate this," Violet said, carefully. With their kind parents dead and Count Olaf treating them so abominably, the three children were not used to kindness from adults, and weren't sure if they were expected to do anything back. "Tomorrow, before we use your library again, Klaus and I would be more than happy to do household chores for you. Sunny isn't really old enough to work, but I'm sure we could find some way she could help you."

Justice Strauss smiled at the three children,

but her eyes were sad. She reached out a hand and put it on Violet's hair, and Violet felt more comforted than she had in some time. "That won't be necessary," Justice Strauss said. "You are always welcome in my home." Then she turned and went into her home, and after a moment of staring after her, the Baudelaire orphans went into theirs.

For most of the afternoon, Violet, Klaus, and Sunny cooked the puttanesca sauce according to the recipe. Violet roasted the garlic and washed and chopped the anchovies. Klaus peeled the tomatoes and pitted the olives. Sunny banged on a pot with a wooden spoon, singing a rather repetitive song she had written herself. And all three of the children felt less miserable than they had since their arrival at Count Olaf's. The smell of cooking food is often a calming one, and the kitchen grew cozy as the sauce simmered, a culinary term which means "cooked over low heat." The three orphans spoke of pleasant memories of their parents and about Justice Strauss, who they agreed was a wonderful neighbor and in whose library they planned to spend a great deal of time. As they talked, they mixed and tasted the chocolate pudding.

Just as they were placing the pudding in the refrigerator to cool, Violet, Klaus, and Sunny heard a loud, booming sound as the front door was flung open, and I'm sure I don't have to tell you who was home.

"Orphans?" Count Olaf called out in his scratchy voice. "Where are you, orphans?"

"In the kitchen, Count Olaf," Klaus called. "We're just finishing dinner."

"You'd better be," Count Olaf said, and strode into the kitchen. He gazed at all three Baudelaire children with his shiny, shiny eyes. "My troupe is right behind me and they are very hungry. Where is the roast beef?"

"We didn't make roast beef," Violet said. "We made puttanesca sauce."

"What?" Count Olaf asked. "No roast beef?"

"You didn't tell us you wanted roast beef," Klaus said.

Count Olaf slid toward the children so that he looked even taller than he was. His eyes grew even brighter, and his one eyebrow raised in anger. "In agreeing to adopt you," he said, "I have become your father, and as your father I am not someone to be trifled with. I demand that you serve roast beef to myself and my guests."

"We don't have any!" Violet cried. "We made puttanesca sauce!"

"*No! No! No!*" Sunny shouted.

Count Olaf looked down at Sunny, who had spoken so suddenly. With an inhuman roar he picked her up in one scraggly hand and raised her so she was staring at him in the eye. Needless to say, Sunny was very frightened and began crying immediately, too scared to even try to bite the hand that held her.

"Put her down immediately, you beast!"

Klaus shouted. He jumped up, trying to rescue Sunny from the grasp of the Count, but he was holding her too high to reach. Count Olaf looked down at Klaus and smiled a terrible, toothy grin, raising the wailing Sunny up even higher in the air. He seemed about to drop her to the floor when there was a large burst of laughter in the next room.

"Olaf! Where's Olaf?" voices called out. Count Olaf paused, still holding the wailing Sunny up in the air, as members of his theater troupe walked into the kitchen. Soon they were crowding the room—an assortment of strange-looking characters of all shapes and sizes. There was a bald man with a very long nose, dressed in a long black robe. There were two women who had bright white powder all over their faces, making them look like ghosts. Behind the women was a man with very long and skinny arms, at the end of which were two hooks instead of hands. There was a person who was extremely fat, and who looked like neither a man nor a woman. And behind this person, standing in the doorway, were an assortment of people the children could not see but who promised to be just as frightening.

"Here you are, Olaf," said one of the white-faced women. "What in the world are you doing?"

"I'm just disciplining these orphans," Count Olaf said. "I asked them to make dinner, and all they have made is some disgusting sauce."

"You can't go easy on children," the man with the hook-hands said. "They must be taught to obey their elders."

The tall, bald man peered at the youngsters. "Are these," he said to Count Olaf, "those wealthy children you were telling me about?"

"Yes," Count Olaf said. "They are so awful I can scarcely stand to touch them." With that, he lowered Sunny, who was still wailing, to the floor. Violet and Klaus breathed a sigh of relief that he had not dropped her from that great height.

"I don't blame you," said someone in the doorway.

Count Olaf rubbed his hands together as if he had been holding something revolting instead of an infant. "Well, enough talk," he said. "I suppose we will eat their dinner, even though it is all wrong. Everyone, follow me to the dining room and I will pour us some wine. Perhaps by the time these brats serve us, we will be too drunk to care if it is roast beef or not."

"Hurrah!" cried several members of the troupe, and they marched through the kitchen, following Count Olaf into the dining room. Nobody paid a bit of attention to the children, except for the bald man, who stopped and stared Violet in the eye.

"You're a pretty one," he said, taking her face in his rough hands. "If I were you I would try not to anger Count Olaf, or he might wreck that pretty little face of yours." Violet shuddered, and the bald man gave a high-pitched giggle and left the room.

The Baudelaire children, alone in the kitchen, found themselves breathing heavily, as if they had just run a long distance. Sunny continued to wail, and Klaus found that his eyes were wet with tears as well. Only Violet didn't cry, but merely trembled with fear and revulsion, a word which here means "an unpleasant mixture of horror and disgust." For several moments none of them could speak.

"This is terrible, terrible," Klaus said finally. "Violet, what can we do?"

"I don't know," she said. "I'm afraid."

"Me too," Klaus said.

"Hux!" Sunny said, as she stopped crying.

"Let's have some dinner!" someone shouted from the dining room, and the theater troupe began pounding on the table in strict rhythm, which is an exceedingly rude thing to do.

"We'd better serve the puttanesca," Klaus said, "or who knows what Count Olaf will do to us."

Violet thought of what the bald man had said, about wrecking her face, and nodded. The two of them looked at the pot of bubbling sauce, which had seemed so cozy while they were making it and now looked like a vat of blood. Then, leaving Sunny behind in the kitchen, they walked into the dining room, Klaus carrying a bowl of the interestingly shaped noodles and Violet carrying the pot of puttanesca sauce and a large ladle with which to serve it. The theater troupe was talking and cackling, drinking again and again from their wine cups and paying no attention to the Baudelaire orphans as they circled the table serving everyone dinner. Violet's right hand ached from holding the heavy ladle. She thought of switching to her left hand, but because she was right-handed she was afraid she might spill the sauce with her left hand, which could enrage Count Olaf again. She stared miserably at Olaf's plate of food and found herself wishing she had bought poison at the market and put it in the puttanesca sauce. Finally, they were through serving, and Klaus and Violet slipped back into the kitchen. They listened to the wild, rough laughter of Count

Olaf and his theater troupe, and they picked at their own portions of food, too miserable to eat. Before long, Olaf's friends were pounding on the table in strict rhythm again, and the orphans went out to the dining room to clear the table, and then again to serve the chocolate pudding. By now it was obvious that Count Olaf and his associates had drunk a great deal of wine, and they slouched at the table and spoke much less. Finally, they roused themselves, and trooped back through the kitchen, scarcely glancing at the children on their way out of the house. Count Olaf looked around the room, which was filled with dirty dishes.

"Because you haven't cleaned up yet," he said to the orphans, "I suppose you can be excused from attending tonight's performance. But after cleaning up, you are to go straight to your beds."

Klaus had been glaring at the floor, trying to hide how upset he was. But at this he could not remain silent. "You mean our *bed*!" he shouted.

"You have only provided us with one bed!"

Members of the theater troupe stopped in their tracks at this outburst, and glanced from Klaus to Count Olaf to see what would happen next. Count Olaf raised his one eyebrow, and his eyes shone bright, but he spoke calmly.

"If you would like another bed," he said, "tomorrow you may go into town and purchase one."

"You know perfectly well we haven't any money," Klaus said.

"Of course you do," Count Olaf said, and his voice began to get a little louder. "You are the inheritors of an enormous fortune."

"That money," Klaus said, remembering what Mr. Poe said, "is not to be used until Violet is of age."

Count Olaf's face grew very red. For a moment he said nothing. Then, in one sudden movement, he reached down and struck Klaus across the face. Klaus fell to the floor, his face inches from the eye tattooed on Olaf's ankle. His glasses leaped from his face and skittered into a corner. His left cheek, where Olaf had struck him, felt as if it were on fire. The theater troupe laughed, and a few of them applauded as if Count Olaf had done something very brave instead of something despicable.

"Come on, friends," Count Olaf said to his comrades. "We'll be late for our own performance."

"If I know you, Olaf," said the man with the hook-hands, "you'll figure out a way to get at that Baudelaire money."

"We'll see," Count Olaf said, but his eyes were shining bright as if he already had an idea. There was another loud boom as the front door shut behind Count Olaf and his terrible friends, and the Baudelaire children were alone in the kitchen. Violet knelt at Klaus's side, giving him a hug to try to make him feel better. Sunny crawled over to his glasses, picked them up, and brought them to him. Klaus began to sob, not so much from the pain but from rage at the terrible situation they were in. Violet and Sunny cried with him, and they continued weeping as they washed the dishes, and as they blew out the candles in the dining room, and as they changed out of their clothes and lay down to go to sleep, Klaus in the bed, Violet on the floor, Sunny on her little cushion of curtains. The moonlight shone through the window, and if anyone had looked into the Baudelaire orphans' bedroom, they would have seen three children crying quietly all night long.

CHAPTER Five

Unless you have been very, very lucky, you have undoubtedly experienced events in your life that have made you cry. So unless you have been very, very lucky, you know that a good, long session of weeping can often make you feel better, even if your circumstances have not changed one bit. So it was with the Baudelaire orphans. Having cried all night, they rose the next morning feeling as if a weight were off their shoulders. The three children knew, of course, that they were still in a terrible situation, but they thought they might do something to make it better.

The morning's note from Count Olaf ordered them to chop firewood in the backyard, and as Violet and Klaus swung the axe down over each log to break it into smaller pieces, they discussed possible plans of action, while Sunny chewed meditatively on a small piece of wood.

"Clearly," Klaus said, fingering the ugly bruise on his face where Olaf had struck him, "we cannot stay here any longer. I would rather take my chances on the streets than live in this terrible place."

"But who knows what misfortunes would befall us on the streets?" Violet pointed out. "At least here we have a roof over our heads."

"I wish our parents' money *could* be used now, instead of when you come of age," Klaus said. "Then we could buy a castle and live in it, with armed guards patrolling the outside to keep out Count Olaf and his troupe."

"And I could have a large inventing studio," Violet said wistfully. She swung the axe down and split a log neatly in two. "Filled with gears and pulleys and wires and an elaborate computer system."

"And I could have a large library," Klaus said, "as comfortable as Justice Strauss's, but more enormous."

"Gibbo!" Sunny shrieked, which appeared to mean "And I could have lots of things to bite."

"But in the meantime," Violet said, "we have to do something about our predicament."

"Perhaps Justice Strauss could adopt us," Klaus said. "She said we were always welcome in her home."

"But she meant for a visit, or to use her library," Violet pointed out. "She didn't mean to *live*."

"Perhaps if we explained our situation to her,

she would agree to adopt us," Klaus said hope-fully, but when Violet looked at him she saw that he knew it was of no use. Adoption is an enormous decision, and not likely to happen impulsively. I'm sure you, in your life, have occasionally wished to be raised by different people than the ones who are raising you, but knew in your heart that the chances of this were very slim.

"I think we should go see Mr. Poe," Violet said. "He told us when he dropped us here that we could contact him at the bank if we had any questions."

"We don't really have a question," Klaus said. "We have a complaint." He was thinking of Mr. Poe walking toward them at Briny Beach, with his terrible message. Even though the fire was of course not Mr. Poe's fault, Klaus was reluc-tant to see Mr. Poe because he was afraid of getting more bad news.

"I can't think of anyone else to contact,"

Violet said. "Mr. Poe is in charge of our affairs, and I'm sure if he knew how horrid Count Olaf is, he would take us right out of here."

Klaus pictured Mr. Poe arriving in his car and putting the Baudelaire orphans inside, to go somewhere else, and felt a stirring of hope. Anywhere would be better than here. "Okay," he said. "Let's get this firewood all chopped and we'll go to the bank."

Invigorated by their plan, the Baudelaire orphans swung their axes at an amazing speed, and soon enough they were done chopping firewood and ready to go to the bank. They remembered Count Olaf saying he had a map of the city, and they looked thoroughly for it, but they couldn't find any trace of a map, and decided it must be in the tower, where they were forbidden to go. So, without directions of any sort, the Baudelaire children set off for the city's banking district in hopes of finding Mr. Poe.

After walking through the meat district, the flower district, and the sculpture district, the three children arrived at the banking district, pausing to take a refreshing sip of water at the Fountain of Victorious Finance. The banking district consisted of several wide streets with large marble buildings on each side of them, all banks. They went first to Trustworthy Bank, and then to Faithful Savings and Loan, and then to Subservient Financial Services, each time inquiring for Mr. Poe. Finally, a receptionist at Subservient said she knew that Mr. Poe worked down the street, at Mulctuary Money Management. The building was square and rather plain-looking, though once inside, the three orphans were intimidated by the hustle and bustle of the people as they raced around the large, echoey room. Finally, they asked a uniformed guard whether they had arrived at the right place to speak to Mr. Poe, and he led them into a large office with many file cabinets and no windows.

"Why, hello," said Mr. Poe, in a puzzled tone

of voice. He was sitting at a desk covered in typed papers that looked important and boring. Surrounding a small framed photograph of his wife and his two beastly sons were three telephones with flashing lights. "Please come in."

"Thank you," said Klaus, shaking Mr. Poe's hand. The Baudelaire youngsters sat down in three large and comfortable chairs.

Mr. Poe opened his mouth to speak, but had to cough into a handkerchief before he could begin. "I'm very busy today," he said, finally. "So I don't have too much time to chat. Next time you should call ahead of time when you plan on being in the neighborhood, and I will put some time aside to take you to lunch."

"That would be very pleasant," Violet said, "and we're sorry we didn't contact you before we stopped by, but we find ourselves in an urgent situation."

"Count Olaf is a madman," Klaus said, getting right to the point. "We cannot stay with him."

"He struck Klaus across the face. See his bruise?" Violet said, but just as she said it, one of the telephones rang, in a loud, unpleasant wail. "Excuse me," Mr. Poe said, and picked up the phone. "Poe here," he said into the receiver. "What? Yes. Yes. Yes. Yes. No. Yes. Thank you." He hung up the phone and looked at the Baudelaires as if he had forgotten they were there.

"I'm sorry," Mr. Poe said, "what were we talking about? Oh, yes, Count Olaf. I'm sorry you don't have a good first impression of him."

"He has only provided us with one bed," Klaus said.

"He makes us do a great many difficult chores."

"He drinks too much wine."

"Excuse me," Mr. Poe said, as another telephone rang. "Poe here," he said. "Seven. Seven. Seven. Seven. Six and a half. Seven. You're welcome." He hung up and quickly wrote something down on one of his papers, then looked at the children. "I'm sorry," he said, "what were you saying about Count Olaf? Making you do chores doesn't sound too bad."

"He calls us orphans."

"He has terrible friends."

"He is always asking about our money."

"Poko!" (This was from Sunny.)

Mr. Poe put up his hands to indicate he had heard enough. "Children, children," he said. "You must give yourselves time to adjust to your new home. You've only been there a few days."

"We have been there long enough to know Count Olaf is a bad man," Klaus said.

Mr. Poe sighed, and looked at each of the three children. His face was kind, but it didn't look like he really believed what the Baudelaire orphans were saying. "Are you familiar with the Latin term 'in loco parentis'?" he asked.

Violet and Sunny looked at Klaus. The biggest reader of the three, he was the most likely to know vocabulary words and foreign phrases. "Something about trains?" he asked. Maybe Mr. Poe was going to take them by train to another relative.

Mr. Poe shook his head. "'In loco parentis' means 'acting in the role of parent,'" he said. "It is a legal term and it applies to Count Olaf. Now that you are in his care, the Count may raise you using any methods he sees fit. I'm sorry if your parents did not make you do any household chores, or if you never saw them drink any wine, or if you like their friends better than Count Olaf's friends, but these are things that you must get used to, as Count Olaf is acting in loco parentis. Understand?"

"But he *struck* my brother!" Violet said. "Look at his face!"

As Violet spoke, Mr. Poe reached into his pocket for his handkerchief and, covering his mouth, coughed many, many times into it. He coughed so loudly that Violet could not be certain he had heard her.

"Whatever Count Olaf has done," Mr. Poe said, glancing down at one of his papers and circling a number, "he has acted in loco parentis, and there's nothing I can do about it. Your money will be well protected by myself and by the bank, but Count Olaf's parenting techniques are his own business. Now, I hate to usher you out posthaste, but I have very much work to do."

The children just sat there, stunned. Mr. Poe looked up, and cleared his throat. "'Posthaste,'" he said, "means—"

"—means you'll do nothing to help us," Violet finished for him. She was shaking with anger and frustration. As one of the phones began ringing, she stood up and walked out of the room, followed by Klaus, who was carrying Sunny. They stalked out of the bank and stood on the street, not knowing what to do next.

"What shall we do next?" Klaus asked sadly.

Violet stared up at the sky. She wished she could invent something that could take them out of there. "It's getting a bit late," she said. "We might as well just go back and think of something else tomorrow. Perhaps we can stop and see Justice Strauss."

"But you said she wouldn't help us," Klaus said.

"Not for help," Violet said, "for books."

It is very useful, when one is young, to learn the difference between "literally" and "figuratively." If something happens literally, it actually happens; if something happens figuratively, it *feels like* it's happening. If you are literally jumping for joy, for instance, it means you are leaping in the air because you are very happy. If you are figuratively jumping for joy, it means you are so happy that you *could* jump for joy, but are saving your energy for other matters. The Baudelaire orphans walked back to Count Olaf's neighborhood and stopped at the home of Justice Strauss, who welcomed them inside and let them choose books from the library. Violet chose several about mechanical inventions,

Klaus chose several about wolves, and Sunny found a book with many pictures of teeth inside. They then went to their room and crowded together on the one bed, reading intently and happily. *Figuratively*, they escaped from Count Olaf and their miserable existence. They did not *literally* escape, because they were still in his house and vulnerable to Olaf's evil in loco parentis ways. But by immersing themselves in their favorite reading topics, they felt far away from their predicament, as if they had escaped. In the situation of the orphans, figuratively escaping was not enough, of course, but at the end of a tiring and hopeless day, it would have to do. Violet, Klaus, and Sunny read their books and, in the back of their minds, hoped that soon their figurative escape would eventually turn into a literal one.

CHAPTER
Six

The next morning, when the children stumbled sleepily from their bedroom into the kitchen, rather than a note from Count Olaf they found Count Olaf himself.

"Good morning, orphans," he said. "I have your oatmeal all ready in bowls for you."

The children took seats at the kitchen table and stared nervously into their oatmeal. If you knew Count Olaf, and he suddenly served you a meal, wouldn't you be afraid there was something terrible in it, like poison or ground glass? But instead, Violet, Klaus, and Sunny found that fresh raspberries had been sprinkled on top of each of their portions. The Baudelaire orphans hadn't had raspberries since their parents died, although they were extremely fond of them.

"Thank you," Klaus said, carefully, picking up one of the raspberries and examining it. Perhaps these were poison berries that just looked like delicious ones. Count Olaf, seeing how suspiciously Klaus was looking at the berries, smiled and plucked a berry out of Sunny's bowl. Looking at each of the three youngsters, he popped it into his mouth and ate it.

"Aren't raspberries delicious?" he asked. "They were my favorite berries when I was your age."

Violet tried to picture Count Olaf as a youngster, but couldn't. His shiny eyes, bony hands, and shadowy smile all seemed to be things only adults possess. Despite her fear of him, however, she took her spoon in her right hand and began to eat her oatmeal. Count Olaf had eaten some, so it probably wasn't poisonous, and

anyway she was very hungry. Klaus began to eat, too, as did Sunny, who got oatmeal and raspberries all over her face.

"I received a phone call yesterday," Count Olaf said, "from Mr. Poe. He told me you children had been to see him."

The children exchanged glances. They had hoped their visit would be taken in confidence, a phrase which here means "kept a secret between Mr. Poe and themselves and not blabbed to Count Olaf."

"Mr. Poe told me," Count Olaf said, "that you appeared to be having some difficulty adjusting to the life I have so graciously provided for you. I'm very sorry to hear that."

The children looked at Count Olaf. His face was very serious, as if he *were* very sorry to hear that, but his eyes were shiny and bright, the way they are when someone is telling a joke.

"Is that so?" Violet said. "I'm sorry Mr. Poe bothered you."

"I'm glad he did," Count Olaf said, "because

I want the three of you to feel at home here, now that I am your father."

The children shuddered a little at that, remembering their own kind father and gazing sadly at the poor substitute now sitting across the table from them.

"Lately," Count Olaf said, "I have been very nervous about my performances with the theater troupe, and I'm afraid I may have acted a bit standoffish."

The word "standoffish" is a wonderful one, but it does not describe Count Olaf's behavior toward the children. It means "reluctant to associate with others," and it might describe somebody who, during a party, would stand in a corner and not talk to anyone. It would *not* describe somebody who provides one bed for three people to sleep in, forces them to do horrible chores, and strikes them across the face. There are many words for people like that, but "standoffish" is not one of them. Klaus knew the word "standoffish" and almost laughed out loud at Olaf's incorrect use of it. But his face still had a bruise on it, so Klaus remained silent.

"Therefore, to make you feel a little more at home here, I would like to have you participate in my next play. Perhaps if you took part in the work I do, you would be less likely to run off complaining to Mr. Poe."

"In what way would we participate?" Violet asked. She was thinking of all the chores they already did for Count Olaf, and was not in the mood to do more.

"Well," Count Olaf said, his eyes shining brightly, "the play is called *The Marvelous Marriage*, and it is written by the great playwright Al Funcoot. We will give only one performance, on this Friday night. It is about a man who is very brave and intelligent, played by me. In the finale, he marries the young, beautiful woman he loves, in front of a crowd of cheering people. *You*, Klaus, and *you*, Sunny, will play some of the cheering people in the crowd."

"But we're shorter than most adults," Klaus said. "Won't that look strange to the audience?"

"You will be playing two midgets who attend the wedding," Olaf said patiently.

"And what will I do?" Violet asked. "I am very handy with tools, so perhaps I could help you build the set."

"Build the set? Heavens, no," Count Olaf said. "A pretty girl like you shouldn't be working backstage."

"But I'd *like* to," Violet said.

Count Olaf's one eyebrow raised slightly, and the Baudelaire orphans recognized this sign of his anger. But then the eyebrow went down again as he forced himself to remain calm. "But I have such an important role for you onstage," he said. "You are going to play the young woman I marry."

Violet felt her oatmeal and raspberries shift around in her stomach as if she had just caught the flu. It was bad enough having Count Olaf acting in loco parentis and announcing himself as their father, but to consider this man her husband, even for the purposes of a play, was even more dreadful.

"It's a *very* important role," he continued, his mouth curling up into an unconvincing smile, "although you have no lines other than 'I do,' which you will say when Justice Strauss asks you if you will have me."

"Justice Strauss?" Violet said. "What does she have to do with it?"

"She has agreed to play the part of the judge," Count Olaf said. Behind him, one of the eyes painted on the kitchen walls closely watched over each of the Baudelaire children. "I asked Justice Strauss to participate because I wanted to be neighborly, as well as fatherly."

"Count Olaf," Violet said, and then stopped herself. She wanted to argue her way out of playing his bride, but she didn't want to make him angry. "*Father*," she said, "I'm not sure I'm talented enough to perform professionally. I would hate to disgrace your good name and the name of Al Funcoot. Plus I'll be very busy in the next few weeks working on my inventions—and learning how to prepare roast beef," she added quickly, remembering how he had behaved about dinner.

Count Olaf reached out one of his spidery hands and stroked Violet on the chin, looking deep into her eyes. *"You will,"* he said, "participate in this theatrical performance. I would prefer it if you would participate voluntarily, but as I believe Mr. Poe explained to you, I can order you to participate and *you must obey."* Olaf's sharp and dirty fingernails gently scratched on Violet's chin, and she shivered. The room was very, very quiet as Olaf finally let go, and stood up and left without a word. The Baudelaire children listened to his heavy footsteps go up the stairs to the tower they were forbidden to enter.

"Well," Klaus said hesitantly, "I guess it won't hurt to be in the play. It seems to be very important to him, and we want to keep on his good side."

"But he must be up to something," Violet said.

"You don't think those berries were poisoned, do you?" Klaus asked worriedly.

"No," Violet said. "Olaf is after the fortune we will inherit. Killing us would do him no good."

"But what good does it do him to have us be in his stupid play?"

"I don't know," Violet admitted miserably. She stood up and started washing out the oatmeal bowls.

"I wish we knew something more about inheritance law," Klaus said. "I'll bet Count Olaf has cooked up some plan to get our money, but I don't know what it could be."

"I guess we could ask Mr. Poe about it," Violet said doubtfully, as Klaus stood beside her and dried the dishes. "He knows all those Latin legal phrases."

"But Mr. Poe would probably call Count Olaf

again, and then he'd know we were on to him,"
Klaus pointed out. "Maybe we should try to talk
to Justice Strauss. She's a judge, so she must
know all about the law."

"But she's also Olaf's neighbor," Violet
replied, "and she might tell him that we had
asked."

Klaus took his glasses off, which he often did
when he was thinking hard. "How could we find
out about the law without Olaf's knowledge?"

"Book!" Sunny shouted suddenly. She probably meant something like "Would somebody
please wipe my face?" but it made Violet and
Klaus look at each other. *Book.* They were both
thinking the same thing: Surely Justice Strauss
would have a book on inheritance law.

"Count Olaf didn't leave us any chores to do,"
Violet said, "so I suppose we are free to visit
Justice Strauss and her library."

Klaus smiled. "Yes indeed," he said. "And
you know, today I don't think I'll choose a book
on wolves."

"Nor I," Violet said, "on mechanical engineering. I think I'd like to read about inheritance law."

"Well, let's go," Klaus said. "Justice Strauss said we could come over soon, and we don't want to be *standoffish*."

At the mention of the word that Count Olaf had used so ridiculously, the Baudelaire orphans all laughed, even Sunny, who of course did not have a very big vocabulary. Swiftly they put away the clean oatmeal bowls in the kitchen cupboards, which watched them with painted eyes. Then the three young people ran next door. Friday, the day of the performance, was only a few days off, and the children wanted to figure out Count Olaf's plan as quickly as possible.

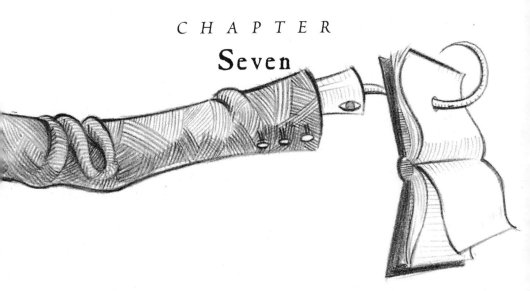

CHAPTER
Seven

There are many, many types of books in the
world, which makes good sense, because there
are many, many types of people, and everybody
wants to read something different. For instance,
people who hate stories in which terrible things
happen to small children should put this book
down immediately. But one type of book that
practically no one likes to read is a book about
the law. Books about the law are notorious for
being very long, very dull, and very difficult to

read. This is one reason many lawyers make heaps of money. The money is an incentive— the word "incentive" here means "an offered reward to persuade you to do something you don't want to do"—to read long, dull, and difficult books.

The Baudelaire children had a slightly different incentive for reading these books, of course. Their incentive was not heaps of money, but preventing Count Olaf from doing something horrible to them in order to get heaps of money. But even with this incentive, getting through the law books in Justice Strauss's private library was a very, very, very hard task.

"Goodness," Justice Strauss said, when she came into the library and saw what they were reading. She had let them in the house but immediately went into the backyard to do her gardening, leaving the Baudelaire orphans alone in her glorious library. "I thought you were interested in mechanical engineering, animals of North America, and teeth. Are you sure you want to read those enormous law books? Even *I* don't like reading them, and I work in law."

"Yes," Violet lied, "I find them very interesting, Justice Strauss."

"So do I," Klaus said. "Violet and I are considering a career in law, so we are fascinated by these books."

"Well," Justice Strauss said, "Sunny can't possibly be interested. Maybe she'd like to come help me with the gardening."

"Wipi!" Sunny shrieked, which meant "I'd much prefer gardening to sitting around watching my siblings struggle through law books."

"Well, make sure she doesn't eat any dirt," Klaus said, bringing Sunny over to the judge.

"Of course," said Justice Strauss. "We wouldn't want her to be sick for the big performance."

Violet and Klaus exchanged a look. "Are you excited about the play?" Violet asked hesitantly.

Justice Strauss's face lit up. "Oh yes," she said. "I've always wanted to perform onstage, ever since I was a little girl. And now Count Olaf has given me the opportunity to live my lifelong dream. Aren't you thrilled to be a part of the theater?"

"I guess so," Violet said.

"Of course you are," Judge Strauss said, stars in her eyes and Sunny in her hands. She left the library and Klaus and Violet looked at each other and sighed.

"She's stagestruck," Klaus said. "She won't believe that Count Olaf is up to something, no matter what."

"She wouldn't help us anyway," Violet pointed out glumly. "She's a judge, and she'd just start babbling about in loco parentis like Mr. Poe."

"That's why we've got to find a legal reason to stop the performance," Klaus said firmly. "Have you found anything in your book yet?"

"Nothing helpful," Violet said, glancing down at a piece of scrap paper on which she had been taking notes. "Fifty years ago there was a woman who left an enormous sum of money to her pet weasel, and none to her three sons. The three sons tried to prove that the woman was insane so the money would go to them."

"What happened?" Klaus asked.

"I think the weasel died," Violet replied, "but I'm not sure. I have to look up some of the words."

"I don't think it's going to help us anyway," Klaus said.

"Maybe Count Olaf is trying to prove that *we're* insane, so he'd get the money," Violet said.

"But why would making us be in *The Marvelous Marriage* prove we were insane?" Klaus asked.

"I don't know," Violet admitted. "I'm stuck. Have you found anything?"

"Around the time of your weasel lady," Klaus said, flipping through the enormous book he had been reading, "a group of actors put on a production of Shakespeare's *Macbeth*, and none of them wore any clothing."

Violet blushed. "You mean they were all naked, onstage?"

"Only briefly," Klaus said, smiling. "The police came and shut down the production. I don't think that's very helpful, either. It was just pretty interesting to read about."

Violet sighed. "Maybe Count Olaf isn't up to anything," she said. "I'm not interested in performing in his play, but perhaps we're all worked up about nothing. Maybe Count Olaf really *is* just trying to welcome us into the family."

"How can you say that?" Klaus cried. "He struck me across the face."

"But there's no way he can get hold of our fortune just by putting us in a play," Violet said. "My eyes are tired from reading these books, Klaus, and they aren't helping us. I'm going to go out and help Justice Strauss in the garden."

Klaus watched his sister leave the library and felt a wave of hopelessness wash over him. The day of the performance was not far off, and he hadn't even figured out what Count Olaf was up to, let alone how to stop him. All his life, Klaus had believed that if you read enough books you could solve any problem, but now he wasn't so sure.

"You there!" A voice coming from the doorway startled Klaus out of his thoughts. "Count Olaf sent me to look for you. You are to return to the house immediately."

Klaus turned and saw one of the members of Count Olaf's theater troupe, the one with hooks for hands, standing in the doorway. "What are you doing in this musty old room, anyway?" he asked in his croak of a voice, walking over to where Klaus was sitting. Narrowing his beady eyes, he read the title of one of the books. "*Inheritance Law and Its Implications*?" he said sharply. "Why are you reading that?"

"Why do you think I'm reading it?" Klaus said.

"I'll tell you what I think." The man put one of his terrible hooks on Klaus's shoulder. "I think you should never be allowed inside this library again, at least until Friday. We don't want a little boy getting big ideas. Now, where is your sister and that hideous baby?"

"In the garden," Klaus said, shrugging the hook off of his shoulder. "Why don't you go and get them?"

The man leaned over until his face was just inches from Klaus's, so close that the man's features flickered into a blur. "Listen to me very carefully, little boy," he said, breathing out foul steam with every word. "The only reason Count Olaf hasn't torn you limb from limb is that he hasn't gotten hold of your money. He allows you to live while he works out his plans. But ask yourself this, you little bookworm: What reason will he have to keep you alive after he has your money? What do you think will happen to you then?"

Klaus felt an icy chill go through him as the horrible man spoke. He had never been so terrified in all his life. He found that his arms and legs were shaking uncontrollably, as if he were having some sort of fit. His mouth was making strange sounds, like Sunny always did, as he struggled to find something to say. "Ah—" Klaus heard himself choke out. "Ah—"

"When the time comes," the hook-handed man said smoothly, ignoring Klaus's noises, "I believe Count Olaf just might leave you to me. So if I were you, I'd start acting a little nicer." The man stood up again and put both his hooks in front of Klaus's face, letting the light from the reading lamps reflect off the wicked-looking devices. "Now, if you will excuse me, I have to fetch your poor orphan siblings."

Klaus felt his body go limp as the hook-handed man left the room, and he wanted to sit there for a moment and catch his breath. But his mind wouldn't let him. This was his last moment in the library, and perhaps his last opportunity to foil Count Olaf's plan. But what to do? Hearing the faint sounds of the hook-handed man talking to Justice Strauss in the garden, Klaus looked frantically around the library for something that could be helpful.

Then, just as he heard the man's footsteps heading back his way, Klaus spied one book, and quickly grabbed it. He untucked his shirt and put the book inside, hastily retucking it just as the hook-handed man reentered the library, escorting Violet and carrying Sunny, who was trying without success to bite the man's hooks.

"I'm ready to go," Klaus said quickly, and walked out the door before the man could get a good look at him. He walked quickly ahead of his siblings, hoping that nobody would notice the book-shaped lump in his shirt. Maybe, just maybe, the book Klaus was smuggling could save their lives.

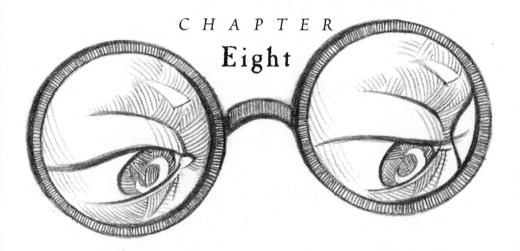

Eight

Klaus stayed up all night reading, which was normally something he loved to do. Back when his parents were alive, Klaus used to take a flashlight to bed with him and hide under the covers, reading until he couldn't keep his eyes open. Some mornings, his father would come into Klaus's room to wake him up and find him asleep, still clutching his flashlight in one hand and his book in the other. But on this particular night, of course, the circumstances were much different.

Klaus stood by the window, squinting as he read his smuggled book by the moonlight that trickled into the room. He occasionally glanced at his sisters. Violet was sleeping fitfully—a word which here means "with much tossing and turning"—on the lumpy bed, and Sunny had wormed her way into the pile of curtains so that she just looked like a small heap of cloth. Klaus had not told his siblings about the book, because he didn't want to give them false hope. He wasn't sure the book would help them out of their dilemma.

The book was long, and difficult to read, and Klaus became more and more tired as the night wore on. Occasionally his eyes would close. He found himself reading the same sentence over and over. He found himself reading the same sentence over and over. He found himself reading the same sentence over and over. But then he would remember the way the hook-hands of Count Olaf's associate had glinted in the library, and would imagine them tearing into his flesh, and he would wake right up and continue reading. He found a small scrap of paper and tore it into strips, which he used to mark significant parts of the book.

By the time the light outside grew gray with the approaching dawn, Klaus had found out all he needed to know. His hopes rose along with the sun. Finally, when the first few birds began to sing, Klaus tiptoed to the door of the bedroom and eased it open quietly, careful not to wake the restless Violet or Sunny, who was still hidden in the pile of curtains. Then he went to the kitchen and sat and waited for Count Olaf.

He didn't have to wait long before he heard Olaf tromping down the tower stairs. When Count Olaf walked into the kitchen, he saw Klaus sitting at the table and smirked, a word which here means "smiled in an unfriendly, phony way."

"Hello, orphan," he said. "You're up early."

Klaus's heart was beating fast, but he felt calm on the outside, as if he had on a layer of invisible armor. "I've been up all night," he said, "reading this book." He put the book out on the table so Olaf could see it. "It's called *Nuptial Law*," Klaus said, "and I learned many interesting things while reading it."

Count Olaf had taken out a bottle of wine to pour himself some breakfast, but when he saw the book he stopped, and sat down.

"The word 'nuptial,'" Klaus said, "means 'relating to marriage.'"

"I *know* what the word means," Count Olaf growled. "Where did you get that book?"

"From Justice Strauss's library," Klaus said. "But that's not important. What's important is that I have found out your plan."

"Is that so?" Count Olaf said, his one eyebrow raising. "And what is my plan, you little runt?"

Klaus ignored the insult and opened the book to where one of the scraps of paper was marking his place. "'The laws of marriage in this community are very simple,'" he read out loud.

"'The requirements are as follows: the presence of a judge, a statement of "I do" by both the bride and the groom, and the signing of an explanatory document in the bride's own hand.'" Klaus put down the book and pointed at Count Olaf. "If my sister says 'I do' and signs a piece of paper, while Justice Strauss is in the room, then she is legally married. This play you're putting on shouldn't be called *The Marvelous Marriage*. It should be called *The Menacing Marriage*. You're not going to marry Violet figuratively—you're going to marry her literally! This play won't be pretend; it will be real and legally binding."

Count Olaf laughed a rough, hoarse laugh. "Your sister isn't old enough to get married."

"She can get married if she has the permission of her legal guardian, acting in loco parentis," Klaus said. "I read that, too. You can't fool me."

"Why in the world would I want to actually marry your sister?" Count Olaf asked. "It is true she is very pretty, but a man like myself can acquire any number of beautiful women."

Klaus turned to a different section of *Nuptial Law*. "'A legal husband,'" he read out loud, "'has the right to control any money in the possession of his legal wife.'" Klaus gazed at Count Olaf in triumph. "You're going to marry my sister to gain control of the Baudelaire fortune! Or at least, that's what you *planned* to do. But when I show this information to Mr. Poe, your play will *not* be performed, and you will go to jail!"

Count Olaf's eyes grew very shiny, but he continued to smirk at Klaus. This was surprising. Klaus had guessed that once he announced what he knew, this dreadful man would have been very angry, even violent. After all, he'd had a furious outburst just because he'd wanted roast beef instead of puttanesca sauce. Surely he'd be even more enraged to have his plan discovered. But Count Olaf just sat there as calmly as if they were discussing the weather.

"I guess you've found me out," Olaf said

simply. "I suppose you're right: I'll go to prison, and you and the other orphans will go free. Now, why don't you run up to your room and wake your sisters? I'm sure they'll want to know all about your grand victory over my evil ways."

Klaus looked closely at Count Olaf, who was continuing to smile as if he had just told a clever joke. Why wasn't he threatening Klaus in anger, or tearing his hair out in frustration, or running to pack his clothes and escape? This wasn't happening at all the way Klaus had pictured it.

"Well, I *will* go tell my sisters," he said, and walked back into his bedroom. Violet was still dozing on the bed and Sunny was still hidden beneath the curtains. Klaus woke Violet up first.

"I stayed up all night reading," Klaus said breathlessly, as his sister opened her eyes, "and I discovered what Count Olaf is up to. He plans to marry you for real, when you and Justice Strauss and everyone all think it's just a play, and once he's your husband he'll have control of our parents' money and he can dispose of us."

"How can he marry me for real?" Violet asked. "It's only a play."

"The only legal requirements of marriage in this community," Klaus explained, holding up *Nuptial Law* to show his sister where he'd learned the information, "are your saying 'I do,' and signing a document in your own hand in the presence of a judge—like Justice Strauss!"

"But surely I'm not old enough to get married," Violet said. "I'm only fourteen."

"Girls under the age of eighteen," Klaus said, flipping to another part of the book, "can marry if they have the permission of their legal guardian. That's Count Olaf."

"Oh no!" Violet cried. "What can we do?"

"We can show this to Mr. Poe," Klaus said, pointing to the book, "and he will finally believe us that Count Olaf is up to no good. Quick, get dressed while I wake up Sunny, and we can be at the bank by the time it opens."

Violet, who usually moved slowly in the mornings, nodded and immediately got out of bed and went to the cardboard box to find some proper clothing. Klaus walked over to the lump of curtains to wake up his younger sister.

"Sunny," he called out kindly, putting his hand on where he thought his sister's head was. "Sunny."

There was no answer. Klaus called out "Sunny" again, and pulled away the top fold of the curtains to wake up the youngest Baudelaire child. "Sunny," he said, but then he stopped. For underneath the curtain was nothing but another curtain. He moved aside all the layers, but his little sister was nowhere to be found. *"Sunny!"* he yelled, looking around the room. Violet dropped the dress she was holding and began to help him search. They looked in every corner, under the bed, and even inside the cardboard box. But Sunny was gone.

"Where can she be?" Violet asked worriedly. "She's not the type to run off."

"Where can she be indeed?" said a voice behind them, and the two children turned around. Count Olaf was standing in the doorway, watching Violet and Klaus as they searched the room. His eyes were shining brighter than they ever had, and he was still smiling like he'd just uttered a joke.

CHAPTER
Nine

"*Yes,*" Count Olaf continued, "it certainly is strange to find a child missing. And one so small, and helpless."

"Where's Sunny?" Violet cried. "What have you done with her?"

Count Olaf continued to speak as if he had not heard Violet. "But then again, one sees strange things every day. In fact, if you two orphans follow me out to the backyard, I think we will all see something rather unusual."

The Baudelaire children didn't say anything, but followed Count Olaf through the house and out the back door. Violet looked around the small, scraggly yard, in which she had not been since she and Klaus had been forced to chop wood. The pile of logs they had made was still lying there untouched, as if Count Olaf had merely made them chop logs for his own amusement, rather than for any purpose. Violet shivered, still in her nightgown, but as she gazed here and there she saw nothing unusual.

"You're not looking in the right place," Count Olaf said. "For children who read so much, you two are remarkably unintelligent."

Violet looked over in the direction of Count Olaf, but could not meet his eyes. The eyes on his face, that is. She was staring at his feet, and could see the tattooed eye that had been watching the Baudelaire orphans since their troubles had begun. Then her eyes traveled up Count Olaf's lean, shabbily dressed body, and she saw that he was pointing up with one scrawny hand. She followed his gesture and found herself looking at the forbidden tower. It was made of dirty stone, with only one lone window, and just barely visible in the window was what looked like a birdcage.

"Oh no," Klaus said in a small, scared voice, and Violet looked again. It *was* a birdcage, dangling from the tower window like a flag in the wind, but inside the birdcage she could see a small and frightened Sunny. When Violet looked closely, she could see there was a large piece of tape across her sister's mouth, and ropes around her body. She was utterly trapped.

"Let her go!" Violet said to Count Olaf. "She has done nothing to you! She is an *infant*!"

"Well, now," Count Olaf said, sitting on a stump. "If you really want me to let her go, I will. But surely even a stupid brat like you might realize that if I let her go—or, more accurately, if I ask my comrade to let her go—poor little Sunny might not survive the fall down to the ground. That's a thirty-foot tower, which is a very long way for a very little person to fall, even when she's inside a cage. But if you insist—"

"*No!*" Klaus cried. "*Don't!*"

Violet looked into Count Olaf's eyes, and then at the small parcel that was her sister, hanging from the top of the tower and moving slowly in the breeze. She pictured Sunny toppling from the tower and onto the ground, pictured her sister's last thoughts being ones of sheer terror. "*Please,*" she said to Olaf, feeling tears in her eyes. "She's just a baby. We'll do *anything, anything.* Just don't harm her."

"*Anything?*" Count Olaf asked, his eyebrow rising. He leaned in toward Violet and gazed into her eyes. "*Anything?* Would you, for instance, consider marrying me during tomorrow night's performance?"

Violet stared at him. She had an odd feeling in her stomach, as if *she* were the one being thrown from a great height. The really frightening thing about Olaf, she realized, was that he was very smart after all. He wasn't merely an unsavory drunken brute, but an unsavory, *clever* drunken brute.

"While you were busy reading books and making accusations," Count Olaf said, "I had one of my quietest, sneakiest assistants skulk into your bedroom and steal little Sunny away. She is perfectly safe, for now. But I consider her to be a stick behind a stubborn mule."

"Our sister is not a stick," Klaus said.

"A stubborn mule," Count Olaf explained, "does not move in the direction its owner wants it to. In that way, it is like you children, who insist on mucking up my plans. Any animal owner will tell you that a stubborn mule will move in the proper direction if there is a carrot in front of it, and a stick behind it. It will move toward the carrot, because it wants the reward of food, and away from the stick, because it does not want the punishment of pain. Likewise, you will do what I say, to avoid the punishment of the loss of your sister, and because you want the reward of surviving this experience. Now, Violet, let me ask you again: *will* you marry me?"

Violet swallowed, and looked down at Count Olaf's tattoo. She could not bring herself to answer.

"Come now," Count Olaf said, his voice faking—a word which here means "feigning"— kindness. He reached out a hand and stroked Violet's hair. "Would it be so terrible to be my bride, to live in my house for the rest of your life? You're such a lovely girl, after the marriage I wouldn't dispose of you like your brother and sister."

Violet imagined sleeping beside Count Olaf, and waking up each morning to look at this terrible man. She pictured wandering around the house, trying to avoid him all day, and cooking for his terrible friends at night, perhaps every night, for the rest of her life. But then she looked up at her helpless sister and knew what her answer must be. "If you let Sunny go," she said finally, "I will marry you."

"I will let Sunny go," Count Olaf answered, "after tomorrow night's performance. In the meantime, she will remain in the tower for safe-keeping. And, as a warning, I will tell you that my assistants will stand guard at the door to the tower staircase, in case you were getting any ideas."

"You're a terrible man," Klaus spat out, but Count Olaf merely smiled again.

"I may be a terrible man," Count Olaf said, "but I have been able to concoct a foolproof way of getting your fortune, which is more than you've been able to do." With that, he began to stride toward the house. "Remember that, orphans," he said. "You may have read more books than I have, but it didn't help you gain the upper hand in this situation. Now, give me that book which gave you such grand ideas, and do the chores assigned to you."

Klaus sighed, and relinquished—a word which here means "gave to Count Olaf even though he didn't want to"—the book on nuptial law. He began to follow Count Olaf into the house, but Violet stayed still as a statue. She hadn't been listening to that last speech of Count Olaf's, knowing it would be full of the usual self-congratulatory nonsense and despicable insults. She was staring at the tower, not at the top, where her sister was dangling, but the whole length of it. Klaus looked back at her and saw something he hadn't seen in quite some time. To those who hadn't been around Violet long, nothing would have seemed unusual, but those who knew her well knew that when she tied her hair up in a ribbon to keep it out of her eyes, it meant that the gears and levers of her inventing brain were whirring at top speed.

CHAPTER
Ten

That night, Klaus was the
Baudelaire orphan sleeping
fitfully in the bed, and Violet
was the Baudelaire orphan
staying up, working by the light
of the moon. All day, the two
siblings had wandered around
the house, doing the assigned
chores and scarcely speaking to
each other. Klaus was too tired
and despondent to speak, and
Violet was holed up in the inventing area of her mind, too
busy planning to talk.

When night approached, Violet gathered up the curtains that had been Sunny's bed and brought them to the door to the tower stairs, where the enormous assistant of Count Olaf's, the one who looked like neither a man nor a woman, was standing guard. Violet asked whether she could bring the blankets to her sister, to make her more comfortable during the night. The enormous creature merely looked at Violet with its blank white eyes and shook its head, then dismissed her with a silent gesture.

Violet knew, of course, that Sunny was too terrified to be comforted by a handful of draperies, but she hoped that she would be allowed a few moments to hold her and tell her that everything would turn out all right. Also, she wanted to do something known in the crime industry as "casing the joint." "Casing the joint" means observing a particular location in order to formulate a plan. For instance, if you are a bank robber—although I hope you aren't—you might go to the bank a few days before you planned to rob it. Perhaps wearing a disguise, you would look around the bank and observe security guards, cameras, and other obstacles, so you could plan how to avoid capture or death during your burglary.

Violet, a law-abiding citizen, was not planning to rob a bank, but she was planning to rescue Sunny, and was hoping to catch a glimpse of the tower room in which her sister was being held prisoner, so as to make her plan more easily. But it appeared that she wasn't going to be able to case the joint after all. This made Violet nervous as she sat on the floor by the window, working on her invention as quietly as she could.

Violet had very few materials with which to invent something, and she didn't want to wander around the house looking for more for fear of arousing the suspicions of Count Olaf and his troupe. But she had enough to build a rescuing device. Above the window was a sturdy metal rod from which the curtains had hung, and

Violet took it down. Using one of the rocks Olaf had left in a pile in the corner, she broke the curtain rod into two pieces. She then bent each piece of the rod into several sharp angles, leaving tiny cuts on her hands as she did so. Then Violet took down the painting of the eye. On the back of the painting, as on the back of many paintings, was a small piece of wire to hang on the hook. She removed the wire and used it to connect the two pieces together. Violet had now made what looked like a large metal spider.

She then went over to the cardboard box and took out the ugliest of the clothes that Mrs. Poe had purchased, the outfits the Baudelaire orphans would never wear no matter how desperate they were. Working quickly and quietly, she began to tear these into long, narrow strips, and to tie these strips together. Among Violet's many useful skills was a vast knowledge of different types of knots. The particular knot she was using was called the Devil's Tongue. A group of female Finnish pirates invented it back in the fifteenth century, and named it the Devil's Tongue because it twisted this way and that, in a most complicated and eerie way. The Devil's Tongue was a very useful knot, and when Violet tied the cloth strips together, end to end, it formed a sort of rope. As she worked, she re-membered something her parents had said to her when Klaus was born, and again when they brought Sunny home from the hospital. "You are the eldest Baudelaire child," they had said, kindly but firmly. "And as the eldest, it will always be your responsibility to look after your younger siblings. Promise us that you will always watch out for them and make sure they don't get into trouble." Violet remembered her promise, and thought of Klaus, whose bruised face still looked sore, and Sunny, dangling from the top of the tower like a flag, and began working faster. Even though Count Olaf was of course the cause of all this misery, Violet felt as if she had broken her promise to her parents, and vowed to make it right.

Eventually, using enough of the ugly clothing, Violet had a rope that was, she hoped, just over thirty feet long. She tied one end of it to the metal spider, and looked at her handiwork. What she had made was called a grappling hook, which is something used for climbing up the sides of buildings, usually for a nefarious purpose. Using the metal end to hook onto something at the top of the tower, and the rope to aid her climb, Violet hoped to reach the top of the tower, untie Sunny's cage, and climb back down. This was, of course, a very risky plan, both because it was dangerous, and because she had made the grappling hook herself, instead of purchasing it at a store that sold such things. But a grappling hook was all Violet could think of to make without a proper inventing laboratory, and time was running short. She hadn't told Klaus about her plan, because she didn't want to give him false hope, so without waking him, she gathered up her grappling hook and tiptoed out of the room.

Once outside, Violet realized her plan was even more difficult than she had thought. The night was quiet, which would mean she would have to make practically no noise at all. The night also had a slight breeze, and when she pictured herself swinging in the breeze, clinging to a rope made of ugly clothing, she almost gave up entirely. And the night was dark, so it was hard to see where she could toss the grappling hook and have the metal arms hook onto something. But, standing there shivering in her nightgown, Violet knew she had to try. Using her right hand, she threw the grappling hook as high and as hard as she could, and waited to see if it would catch onto something.

Clang! The hook made a loud noise as it hit the tower, but it didn't stick to anything, and came crashing back down. Her heart pounding, Violet stood stock-still, wondering if Count Olaf or one of his accomplices would come and investigate. But nobody arrived after a few moments, and Violet, swinging the hook over her head like a lasso, tried again.

Clang! Clang! The grappling hook hit the tower twice as it bounced back down to the ground. Violet waited again, listening for footsteps, but all she heard was her own terrified pulse. She decided to try one more time.

Clang! The grappling hook hit the tower, and fell down again, hitting Violet hard in the shoulder. One of the arms tore her nightgown and cut through her skin. Biting down on her hand to keep from crying out in pain, Violet felt the place in her shoulder where she had been struck, and it was wet with blood. Her arm throbbed in pain.

At this point in the proceedings, if I were Violet, I would have given up, but just as she was about to turn around and go inside the house, she pictured how scared Sunny must be, and, ignoring the pain in her shoulder, Violet used her right hand to throw the hook again.

Cla— The usual *clang!* sound stopped
halfway through, and Violet saw in the dim light
of the moon that the hook wasn't falling.
Nervously, she gave the rope a good yank, and
it stayed put. The grappling hook had worked!

Her feet touching the side of the stone tower
and her hands grasping the rope, Violet closed
her eyes and began to climb. Never daring to
look around, she pulled herself up the tower,
hand over hand, all the time keeping in mind
her promise to her parents and the horrible
things Count Olaf would do if his villainous plan
worked. The evening wind blew harder and
harder as she climbed higher and higher, and
several times Violet had to stop climbing as the
rope moved in the wind. She was certain that at
any moment the cloth would tear, or the hook
would slip, and Violet would be sent tumbling
to her death. But thanks to her adroit inventing
skills—the word "adroit" here means "skillful"—
everything worked the way it was supposed to
work, and suddenly Violet found herself feeling

a piece of metal instead of a cloth rope. She opened her eyes and saw her sister Sunny, who was looking at her frantically and trying to say something past the strip of tape. Violet had arrived at the top of the tower, right at the window where Sunny was tied.

The eldest Baudelaire orphan was about to grab her sister's cage and begin her descent when she saw something that made her stop. It was the spidery end of the grappling hook, which after several attempts had finally stuck onto something on the tower. Violet had guessed, during her climb, that it had found some notch in the stone, or part of the window, or perhaps a piece of furniture inside the tower room, and stuck there. But that wasn't what the hook had stuck on. Violet's grappling hook had stuck on another hook. It was one of the hooks on the hook-handed man. And his other hook, Violet saw, was glinting in the moonlight as it reached right toward her.

CHAPTER
Eleven

"*How* pleasant that you could join us," the hook-handed man said in a sickly sweet voice. Violet immediately tried to scurry back down the rope, but Count Olaf's assistant was too quick for her. In one movement he hoisted her into the tower room and, with a flick of his hook, sent her rescue device clanging to the ground. Now Violet was as trapped as her sister. "I'm so glad you're here," the hook-handed man

said. "I was just thinking how much I wanted to see your pretty face. Have a seat."

"What are you going to do with me?" Violet asked.

"I said *have a seat*!" the hook-handed man snarled, and pushed her into a chair.

Violet looked around the dim and messy room. I am certain that over the course of your own life, you have noticed that people's rooms reflect their personalities. In my room, for instance, I have gathered a collection of objects that are important to me, including a dusty accordion on which I can play a few sad songs, a large bundle of notes on the activities of the Baudelaire orphans, and a blurry photograph, taken a very long time ago, of a woman whose name is Beatrice. These are items that are very precious and dear to me. The tower room held objects that were very dear and precious to Count Olaf, and they were terrible things. There were scraps of paper on which he had written his evil ideas in an illegible scrawl, lying in messy piles on top of the copy of *Nuptial Law* he had taken away from Klaus. There were a few chairs and a handful of candles which were giving off flickering shadows. Littered all over the floor were empty wine bottles and dirty dishes. But most of all were the drawings and paintings and carvings of eyes, big and small, all over the room. There were eyes painted on the ceilings, and scratched into the grimy wooden floors. There were eyes scrawled along the windowsill, and one big eye painted on the knob of the door that led to the stairs. It was a terrible place.

The hook-handed man reached into a pocket of his greasy overcoat and pulled out a walkie-talkie. With some difficulty, he pressed a button and waited a moment. "Boss, it's me," he said. "Your blushing bride just climbed up here to try and rescue the biting brat." He paused as Count Olaf said something. "I don't know. With some sort of rope."

"It was a grappling hook," Violet said, and

tore off a sleeve of her nightgown to make a bandage for her shoulder. "I made it myself."

"She says it was a grappling hook," the hook-handed man said into the walkie-talkie. "I don't know, boss. Yes, boss. Yes, boss, of course I under-stand she's *yours*. Yes, boss." He pressed a button to disconnect the line, and then turned to face Violet. "Count Olaf is very displeased with his bride."

"I'm not his bride," Violet said bitterly.

"Very soon you will be," the hook-handed man said, wagging his hook the way most people would wag a finger. "In the meantime, however, I have to go and fetch your brother. The three of you will be locked in this room until night falls. That way, Count Olaf can be sure you will all stay out of mischief." With that, the hook-handed man stomped out of the room. Violet heard the door lock behind him, and then listened to his footsteps fading away down the stairs. She immediately went over to Sunny, and put a hand on her little head. Afraid to untie or untape her sister for fear of incurring—a word which here means "bringing about"—Count Olaf's wrath, Violet stroked Sunny's hair and murmured that everything was all right.

But of course, everything was *not* all right. Everything was all wrong. As the first light of morning trickled into the tower room, Violet reflected on all the awful things she and her siblings had experienced recently. Their parents had died, suddenly and horribly. Mrs. Poe had bought them ugly clothing. They had moved into Count Olaf's house and were treated terribly. Mr. Poe had refused to help them. They had discovered a fiendish plot involving marrying Violet and stealing the Baudelaire fortune. Klaus had tried to confront Olaf with knowledge he'd learned in Justice Strauss's library and failed. Poor Sunny had been captured. And now, Violet had tried to rescue Sunny and found herself captured as well. All in all, the Baudelaire orphans had encountered catastrophe after catastrophe, and Violet found their situation lamentably deplorable, a phrase which here means "it was not at all enjoyable."

The sound of footsteps coming up the stairs brought Violet out of her thoughts, and soon the hook-handed man opened the door and thrust a very tired, confused, and scared Klaus into the room.

"Here's the last orphan," the hook-handed man said. "And now, I must go help Count Olaf with final preparations for tonight's performance. No monkey business, you two, or I will have to tie you up and let you dangle out of the window as well." Glaring at them, he locked the door again and tromped downstairs.

Klaus blinked and looked around the filthy room. He was still in his pajamas. "What has happened?" he asked Violet. "Why are we up here?"

"I tried to rescue Sunny," Violet said, "using an invention of mine to climb up the tower."

Klaus went over to the window and looked down at the ground. "It's so high up," he said.

"You must have been terrified."

"It was very scary," she admitted, "but not as scary as the thought of marrying Count Olaf."

"I'm sorry your invention didn't work," Klaus said sadly.

"The invention worked fine," Violet said, rubbing her sore shoulder. "I just got caught. And now we're doomed. The hook-handed man said he'd keep us here until tonight, and then it's *The Marvelous Marriage.*"

"Do you think you could invent something that would help us escape?" Klaus asked, looking around the room.

"Maybe," Violet said. "And why don't you go through those books and papers? Perhaps there's some information that could be of use."

For the next few hours, Violet and Klaus searched the room and their own minds for anything that might help them. Violet looked for objects with which she could invent something. Klaus read through Count Olaf's papers and books. From time to time, they would go over to Sunny and smile at her, and pat her head, to reassure her. Occasionally, Violet and Klaus would speak to each other, but mostly they were silent, lost in their own thoughts.

"If we had any kerosene," Violet said, around noon, "I could make Molotov cocktails with these bottles."

"What are Molotov cocktails?" Klaus asked.

"They're small bombs made inside bottles," Violet explained. "We could throw them out the window and attract the attention of passersby."

"But we don't have any kerosene," Klaus said mournfully.

They were silent for several hours.

"If we were polygamists," Klaus said, "Count Olaf's marriage plan wouldn't work."

"What are polygamists?" Violet asked.

"Polygamists are people who marry more than one person,'" Klaus explained. "In this community, polygamists are breaking the law, even if they have married in the presence of a judge, with the statement of 'I do' and the signed document in their own hand. I read it here in *Nuptial Law*."

"But we're not polygamists," Violet said mournfully.

They were silent for several *more* hours.

"We could break these bottles in half," Violet said, "and use them as knives, but I'm afraid that Count Olaf's troupe would overpower us."

"You could say 'I don't' instead of 'I do,'" Klaus said, "but I'm afraid Count Olaf would order Sunny dropped off the tower."

"I certainly would," Count Olaf said, and the children jumped. They had been so involved in their conversation that they hadn't heard him come up the stairs and open the door. He was wearing a fancy suit and his eyebrow had been waxed so it looked as shiny as his eyes. Behind him stood the hook-handed man, who smiled and waved a hook at the youngsters. "Come, orphans," Count Olaf said. "It is time for the big event. My associate here will stay behind in this room, and we will keep in constant contact through our walkie-talkies. If *anything* goes wrong during tonight's performance, your sister will be dropped to her death. Come along now."

Violet and Klaus looked at each other, and then at Sunny, still dangling in her cage, and followed Count Olaf out the door. As Klaus walked down the tower stairs, he felt a heavy sinking in his heart as all hope left him. There truly seemed to be no way out of their predicament. Violet was feeling the same way, until she reached out with her right hand to grasp the banister, for balance. She looked at her right hand for a second, and began to think. All the way down the stairs, and out the door, and the short walk down the block to the theater, Violet thought and thought and thought, harder than she had in her entire life.

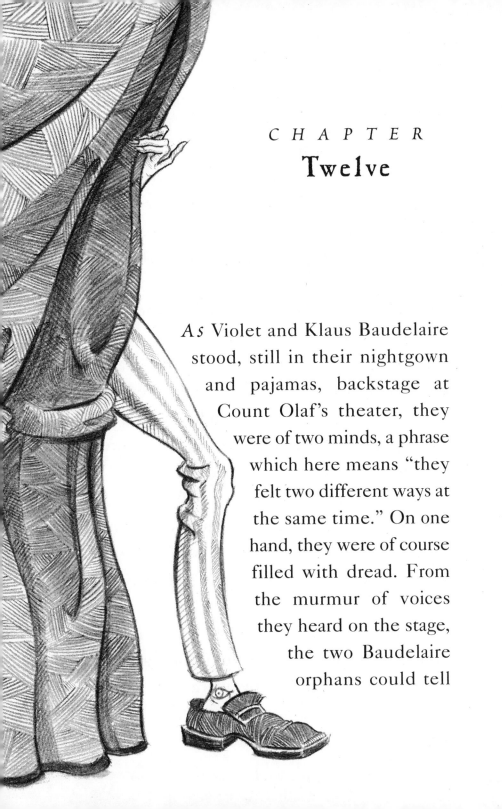

As Violet and Klaus Baudelaire
stood, still in their nightgown
and pajamas, backstage at
Count Olaf's theater, they
were of two minds, a phrase
which here means "they
felt two different ways at
the same time." On one
hand, they were of course
filled with dread. From
the murmur of voices
they heard on the stage,
the two Baudelaire
orphans could tell

that the performance of *The Marvelous Marriage* had begun, and it seemed too late to do anything to foil Count Olaf's plan. On the other hand, however, they were fascinated, as they had never been backstage at a theatrical production and there was so much to see. Members of Count Olaf's theater troupe hurried this way and that, too busy to even glance at the children. Three very short men were carrying a large flat piece of wood, painted to look like a living room. The two white-faced women were arranging flowers in a vase that from far away appeared to be marble, but close up looked more like cardboard. An important-looking man with warts all over his face was adjusting enormous light fixtures. As the children peeked onstage, they could see Count Olaf, in his fancy suit, declaiming some lines from the play, just as the curtain came down, controlled by a woman with very short hair who was pulling on a long rope, attached to a pulley. Despite their fear, you see, the two older Baudelaires were very interested in what was going on, and only wished that they were not involved in any way.

As the curtain fell, Count Olaf strode offstage and looked at the children. "It's the end of Act Two! Why aren't the orphans in their costumes?" he hissed to the two white-faced women. Then, as the audience broke into applause, his angry expression turned to one of joy, and he walked back onstage. Gesturing to the short-haired woman to raise the curtain, he strode to the exact center of the stage and took elaborate bows as the curtain came up. He waved and blew kisses to the audience as the curtain came down again, and then his face once again filled with anger. "Intermission is only ten minutes," he said, "and then the children must perform. Get them into costumes, quickly!"

Without a word the two white-faced women grabbed Violet and Klaus by the wrists and led them into a dressing room. The room was dusty but shiny, covered in mirrors and tiny lights so the actors could see better to put on their

makeup and wigs, and there were people calling out to one another and laughing as they
changed their clothes. One white-faced woman
yanked Violet's arms up and pulled her nightgown off over her head, and thrust a dirty, lacy
white dress at her to put on. Klaus, meanwhile,
had his pajamas removed by the other white-
faced woman, and was hurriedly stuffed into a
blue sailor suit that itched and made him look
like a toddler.

"Isn't this exciting?" said a voice, and the
children turned to see Justice Strauss, all
dressed up in her judge's robes and powdered
wig. She was clutching a small book. "You children look wonderful!"

"So do you," Klaus said. "What's that book?"

"Why, those are my lines," Justice Strauss
said. "Count Olaf told me to bring a law book
and read the real wedding ceremony, in order to
make the play as realistic as possible. All *you*
have to say, Violet, is 'I do,' but I have to make

quite a speech. This is going to be such fun."

"You know what would be fun," Violet said carefully, "is if you changed your lines around, just a little."

Klaus's face lit up. "Yes, Justice Strauss. Be creative. There's no reason to stick to the legal ceremony. It's not as if it's a real wedding."

Justice Strauss frowned. "I don't know about that, children," she said. "I think it would be best to follow Count Olaf's instructions. After all, he's in charge."

"Justice Strauss!" a voice called. "Justice Strauss! Please report to the makeup artist!"

"Oh my word! I get to wear makeup." Justice Strauss had on a dreamy expression, as if she were about to be crowned queen, instead of just having some powders and creams smeared on her face. "Children, I must go. See you onstage, my dears!"

Justice Strauss ran off, leaving the children to finish changing into their costumes. One of the white-faced women put a flowered headdress on Violet, who realized in horror that the dress she had changed into was a bridal gown. The other woman put a sailor cap on Klaus, who gazed in one of the mirrors, astonished at how ugly he looked. His eyes met those of Violet, who was looking in the mirror as well.

"What can we do?" Klaus said quietly. "Pretend to be sick? Maybe they'd call off the performance."

"Count Olaf would know what we were up to," Violet replied glumly.

"Act Three of *The Marvelous Marriage* by Al Funcoot is about to begin!" a man with a clipboard shouted. "Everyone, please, get in your places for Act Three!"

The actors rushed out of the room, and the white-faced women grabbed the children and hustled them out after them. The backstage area was in complete pandemonium—a word which here means "actors and stagehands running around attending to last-minute details." The bald man with the long nose hurried by the children, then stopped himself, looked at Violet in her wedding dress, and smirked.

"No funny stuff," he said to them, waggling a bony finger. "Remember, when you go out there, just do exactly what you're supposed to do. Count Olaf will be holding his walkie-talkie during the entire act, and if you do even *one thing* wrong, he'll be giving Sunny a call up there in the tower."

"Yes, yes," Klaus said bitterly. He was tired of being threatened in the same way, over and over.

"You'd better do exactly as planned," the man said again.

"I'm sure they will," said a voice suddenly, and the children turned to see Mr. Poe, dressed very formally and accompanied by his wife. He smiled at the children and came over to shake their hands. "Polly and I just wanted to tell you to break a leg."

"What?" Klaus said, alarmed.

"That's a theater term," Mr. Poe explained, "meaning 'good luck on tonight's performance.' I'm glad that you children have adjusted to life with your new father and are participating in family activities."

"Mr. Poe," Klaus said quickly, "Violet and I have something to tell you. It's very important."

"What is it?" Mr. Poe said.

"Yes," said Count Olaf, "what is it you have to tell Mr. Poe, children?"

Count Olaf had appeared, seemingly out of nowhere, and his shiny eyes glared at the children meaningfully. In one hand, Violet and Klaus could see, he held a walkie-talkie.

"Just that we appreciate all you've done for us, Mr. Poe," Klaus said weakly. "That's all we wanted to say."

"Of course, of course," Mr. Poe said, patting him on the back. "Well, Polly and I had better take our seats. Break a leg, Baudelaires!"

"I wish we *could* break a leg," Klaus whispered to Violet, and Mr. Poe left.

"You will, soon enough," Count Olaf said, pushing the two children toward the stage. Other actors were milling about, finding their places for Act Three, and Justice Strauss was off in a corner, practicing her lines from her law book. Klaus took a look around the stage, wondering if anyone there could help. The bald man with the long nose took Klaus's hand and led him to one side.

"You and I will stand *here* for the duration of the act. That means the whole thing."

"I *know* what the word 'duration' means," Klaus said.

"No nonsense," the bald man said. Klaus watched his sister in her wedding gown take her place next to Count Olaf as the curtain rose. Klaus heard applause from the audience as Act Three of *The Marvelous Marriage* began.

It will be of no interest to you if I describe the action of this insipid—the word "insipid" here means "dull and foolish"—play by Al Funcoot, because it was a dreadful play and of no real importance to our story. Various actors and actresses performed very dull dialogue and moved around the set, as Klaus tried to make eye contact with them and see if they would help. He soon realized that this play must have been chosen merely as an excuse for Olaf's evil plan, and not for its entertainment value, as he sensed the audience losing interest and moving around in their seats. Klaus turned his attention to the audience to see whether any of them would notice that something was afoot, but the way the wart-faced man had arranged the lights prevented Klaus from seeing the faces in the auditorium, and he could only make out the dim outlines of the people in the audience. Count Olaf had a great number of very long speeches, which he performed with elaborate gestures and facial expressions. No one seemed to notice that he held a walkie-talkie the entire time.

Finally, Justice Strauss began speaking, and Klaus saw that she was reading directly from the legal book. Her eyes were sparkling and her face flushed as she performed onstage for the first time, too stagestruck to realize she was a part of Olaf's plan. She spoke on and on about Olaf and Violet caring for each other in sickness and in health, in good times and bad, and all of those things that are said to many people who decide, for one reason or another, to get married.

When she finished her speech, Justice Strauss turned to Count Olaf and asked, "Do you take this woman to be your lawfully wedded wife?"

"I do," Count Olaf said, smiling. Klaus saw Violet shudder.

"Do *you*," Justice Strauss said, turning to Violet, "take this man to be your lawfully wedded husband?"

"I do," Violet said. Klaus clenched his fists. His sister had said "I do" in the presence of a judge. Once she signed the official document. the wedding was legally valid. And now, Klaus could see that Justice Strauss was taking the

document from one of the other actors and holding it out to Violet to sign.

"Don't move an inch," the bald man mut-
tered to Klaus, and Klaus thought of poor
Sunny, dangling at the top of the tower, and
stood still as he watched Violet take a long quill
pen from Count Olaf. Violet's eyes were wide
as she looked down at the document, and her
face was pale, and her left hand was trembling
as she signed her name.

CHAPTER
Thirteen

"*And* now, ladies and gentlemen," Count Olaf said, stepping forward to address the audience, "I have an announcement. There is no reason to continue tonight's performance, for its purpose has been served. This has not been a scene of fiction. My marriage to Violet Baudelaire is perfectly legal, and now I am in control of her entire fortune."

There were gasps from the audience, and some of the actors looked at one another in shock. Not everyone, apparently, had known about Olaf's plan. "That can't be!" Justice Strauss cried.

"The marriage laws in this community are quite simple," Count Olaf said. "The bride must say 'I do' in the presence of a judge like yourself, and sign an explanatory document. And all of you"—here Count Olaf gestured out to the audience—"are witnesses."

"But Violet is only a child!" one of the actors said. "She's not old enough to marry."

"She is if her legal guardian agrees," Count Olaf said, "and in addition to being her husband, I am her legal guardian."

"But that piece of paper is not an official document!" Justice Strauss said. "That's just a stage prop!"

Count Olaf took the paper from Violet's hand and gave it to Justice Strauss. "I think if you

look at it closely you will see it is an official document from City Hall."

Justice Strauss took the document in her
hand and read it quickly. Then, closing her eyes,
she sighed deeply and furrowed her brow,
thinking hard. Klaus watched her and wondered
if this were the expression Justice Strauss had
on her face whenever she was serving on the
High Court. "You're right," she said finally, to
Count Olaf, "this marriage, unfortunately, is
completely legal. Violet said 'I do,' and signed
her name here on this paper. Count Olaf, you
are Violet's husband, and therefore in complete
control of her estate."

"That can't be!" said a voice from the audience, and Klaus recognized it as the voice of Mr.
Poe. He ran up the stairs to the stage and took
the document from Justice Strauss. "This is
dreadful nonsense."

"I'm afraid this dreadful nonsense is the law,"
Justice Strauss said. Her eyes were filling up

with tears. "I can't believe how easily I was tricked," she said. "I would never do anything to harm you children. *Never.*"

"You *were* easily tricked," Count Olaf said, grinning, and the judge began to cry. "It was child's play, winning this fortune. Now, if all of you will excuse me, my bride and I need to go home for our wedding night."

"First let Sunny go!" Klaus burst out. "You promised to let her go!"

"Where is Sunny?" Mr. Poe asked.

"She's all tied up at the moment," Count Olaf said, "if you will pardon a little joke." His eyes shone as he pressed buttons on the walkie-talkie, and waited while the hook-handed man answered. "Hello? Yes, of course it's me, you idiot. Everything has gone according to plan. Please remove Sunny from her cage and bring her directly to the theater. Klaus and Sunny have some chores to do before they go to bed." Count Olaf gave Klaus a sharp look. "Are you satisfied now?" he asked.

"Yes," Klaus said quietly. He wasn't satisfied at all, of course, but at least his baby sister was no longer dangling from a tower.

"Don't think you're so safe," the bald man whispered to Klaus. "Count Olaf will take care of you and your sisters later. He doesn't want to do it in front of all these people." He did not have to explain to Klaus what he meant by the phrase "take care of."

"Well, I'm not satisfied *at all*," Mr. Poe said. "This is absolutely horrendous. This is completely monstrous. This is financially dreadful."

"I'm afraid, however," Count Olaf said, "that it is legally binding. Tomorrow, Mr. Poe, I shall come down to the bank and withdraw the complete Baudelaire fortune."

Mr. Poe opened his mouth as if to say something, but began to cough instead. For several seconds he coughed into a handkerchief while everyone waited for him to speak. "I won't allow it," Mr. Poe finally gasped, wiping his mouth. "I absolutely will not allow it."

"I'm afraid you have to," Count Olaf replied.

"I'm—I'm afraid Olaf is right," Justice Strauss said, through her tears. "This marriage is legally binding."

"Begging your pardon," Violet said suddenly, "but I think you may be wrong."

Everyone turned to look at the eldest Baudelaire orphan.

"What did you say, Countess?" Olaf said.

"I'm *not* your countess," Violet said testily, a word which here means "in an extremely annoyed tone." "At least, I don't *think* I am."

"And why is that?" Count Olaf said.

"I did not sign the document in my own hand, as the law states," Violet said.

"What do you mean? We all saw you!" Count Olaf's eyebrow was beginning to rise in anger.

"I'm afraid your husband is right, dear," Justice Strauss said sadly. "There's no use denying it. There are too many witnesses."

"Like most people," Violet said, "I am right-handed. But I signed the document with my left hand."

"*What?*" Count Olaf cried. He snatched the paper from Justice Strauss and looked down at it. His eyes were shining very bright. "You are a *liar*!" he hissed at Violet.

"No she's not," Klaus said excitedly. "I remember, because I watched her left hand trembling as she signed her name."

"It is impossible to prove," Count Olaf said.

"If you like," Violet said, "I shall be happy to sign my name again, on a separate sheet of paper, with my right hand and then with my left. Then we can see which signature the one on the document most resembles."

"A small detail, like which hand you used to sign," Count Olaf said, "doesn't matter in the least."

"If you don't mind, sir," Mr. Poe said, "I'd like Justice Strauss to make that decision."

Everyone looked at Justice Strauss, who was

wiping away the last of her tears. "Let me see," she said quietly, and closed her eyes again. She sighed deeply, and the Baudelaire orphans, and all who liked them, held their breath as Justice Strauss furrowed her brow, thinking hard on the situation. Finally, she smiled. "If Violet is indeed right-handed," she said carefully, "and she signed the document with her left hand, then it follows that the signature does not fulfill the requirements of the nuptial laws. The law clearly states the document must be signed in the bride's *own hand*. Therefore, we can conclude that this marriage is invalid. Violet, you are *not* a countess, and Count Olaf, you are *not* in control of the Baudelaire fortune."

"Hooray!" cried a voice from the audience, and several people applauded. Unless you are a lawyer, it will probably strike you as odd that Count Olaf's plan was defeated by Violet signing with her left hand instead of her right. But the law is an odd thing. For instance, one country in Europe has a law that requires all its bakers to sell bread at the exact same price. A certain island has a law that forbids anyone from removing its fruit. And a town not too far from where you live has a law that bars me from coming within five miles of its borders. Had Violet signed the marriage contract with her right hand, the law would have made her a miserable contessa, but because she signed it with her left, she remained, to her relief, a miserable orphan.

What was good news to Violet and her siblings, of course, was bad news to Count Olaf. Nevertheless, he gave everyone a grim smile. "In that case," he said to Violet, pushing a button on the walkie-talkie, "you will either marry me again, and correctly this time, or I will—"

"Neepo!" Sunny's unmistakable voice rang out over Count Olaf's as she tottered onstage toward her siblings. The hook-handed man followed behind her, his walkie-talkie buzzing and crackling. Count Olaf was too late.

"Sunny! You're safe!" Klaus cried, and

embraced her. Violet rushed over and the two older Baudelaires fussed over the youngest one.

"Somebody bring her something to eat," Violet said. "She must be very hungry after hanging in a tower window all that time."

"Cake!" Sunny shrieked.

"*Argh!*" Count Olaf roared. He began to pace back and forth like an animal in a cage, pausing only to point a finger at Violet. "You may not be my wife," he said, "but you are still my daughter, and—"

"Do you honestly think," Mr. Poe said in an exasperated voice, "that I will allow you to continue to care for these three children, after the treachery I have seen here tonight?"

"The orphans are mine," Count Olaf insisted, "and with me they shall stay. There is nothing illegal about trying to marry someone."

"But there *is* something illegal about dangling an infant out of a tower window," Justice Strauss said indignantly. "You, Count Olaf, will go to jail, and the three children will live with me."

"Arrest him!" a voice said from the audience, and other people took up the cry.

"Send him to jail!"

"He's an evil man!"

"And give us our money back! It was a lousy play!"

Mr. Poe took Count Olaf's arm and, after a brief eruption of coughs, announced in a harsh voice, "I hereby arrest you in the name of the law."

"Oh, Justice Strauss!" Violet said. "Did you really mean what you said? Can we really live with you?"

"Of course I mean it," Justice Strauss said. "I am very fond of you children, and I feel responsible for your welfare."

"Can we use your library every day?" Klaus asked.

"Can we work in the garden?" Violet asked.

"Cake!" Sunny shrieked again, and everyone laughed.

At this point in the story, I feel obliged to interrupt and give you one last warning. As I said at the very beginning, the book you are holding in your hands does not have a happy ending. It may appear now that Count Olaf will go to jail and that the three Baudelaire youngsters will live happily ever after with Justice Strauss, but it is not so. If you like, you may shut the book this instant and not read the unhappy ending that is to follow. You may spend the rest of your life believing that the Baudelaires triumphed over Count Olaf and lived the rest of their lives in the house and library of Justice Strauss, but that is not how the story goes. For as everyone was laughing at Sunny's cry for cake, the important-looking man with all the warts on his face was sneaking toward the controls for the lighting of the theater.

Quick as a wink, the man flicked the main switch so that all the lights went off and every-

one was standing in darkness. Instantly, pandemonium ensued as everyone ran this way and
that, shouting at one another. Actors tripped
over members of the audience. Members of the
audience tripped over theatrical props. Mr. Poe
grabbed his wife, thinking it was Count Olaf.
Klaus grabbed Sunny and held her up as high
as he could, so she wouldn't get hurt. But Violet
knew at once what had happened, and made her
way carefully to where she remembered the
lights had been. When the play was being performed, Violet had watched the light controls
carefully, taking mental notes in case these
devices came in handy for an invention. She was
certain if she could find the switch she could
turn it back on. Her arms stretched in front of
her as if she were blind, Violet made her way
across the stage, stepping carefully around
pieces of furniture and startled actors. In the
darkness, Violet looked like a ghost, her white
wedding gown moving slowly across the stage.
Then, just as she had reached the switch, Violet

felt a hand on her shoulder. A figure leaned in to whisper into her ear.

"I'll get my hands on your fortune if it's the last thing I do," the voice hissed. "And when I have it, I'll kill you and your siblings with my own two hands."

Violet gave a little cry of terror, but flicked the switch on. The entire theater was flooded with light. Everyone blinked and looked around. Mr. Poe let go of his wife. Klaus put Sunny down. But nobody was touching Violet's shoulder. Count Olaf was gone.

"Where did he go?" Mr. Poe shouted. "Where did they *all* go?"

The Baudelaire youngsters looked around and saw that not only had Count Olaf vanished, but his accomplices—the wart-faced man, the hook-handed man, the bald man with the long nose, the enormous person who looked like neither a man nor a woman, and the two white-faced women—had vanished along with him.

"They must have run outside," Klaus said, "while it was still dark."

Mr. Poe led the way outside, and Justice Strauss and the children followed. Way, way down the block, they could see a long black car driving away into the night. Maybe it contained Count Olaf and his associates. Maybe it didn't. But in any case, it turned a corner and disappeared into the dark city as the children watched without a word.

"Blast it," Mr. Poe said. "They're gone. But don't worry, children, we'll catch them. I'm going to go call the police immediately."

Violet, Klaus, and Sunny looked at one another and knew that it wasn't as simple as Mr. Poe said. Count Olaf would take care to stay out of sight as he planned his next move. He was far too clever to be captured by the likes of Mr. Poe.

"Well, let's go home, children," Justice Strauss said. "We can worry about this in the morning, when I've fixed you a good breakfast."

Mr. Poe coughed. "Wait a minute," he said,

looking down at the floor. "I'm sorry to tell you this, children, but I cannot allow you to be raised by someone who is not a relative."

"What?" Violet cried. "After all Justice Strauss has done for us?"

"We never would have figured out Count Olaf's plan without her and her library," Klaus said. "Without Justice Strauss, we would have lost our lives."

"That may be so," Mr. Poe said, "and I thank Justice Strauss for her generosity, but your parents' will is very specific. You must be adopted by a relative. Tonight you will stay with me in my home, and tomorrow I shall go to the bank and figure out what to do with you. I'm sorry, but that is the way it is."

The children looked at Justice Strauss, who sighed heavily and hugged each of the Baudelaire youngsters in turn. "Mr. Poe is right," she said sadly. "He must respect your parents' wishes. Don't you want to do what your parents wanted, children?"

Violet, Klaus, and Sunny pictured their loving parents, and wished more than ever that the fire had not occurred. Never, never had they felt so alone. They wanted very badly to live with this kind and generous woman, but they knew that it simply could not be done. "I guess you're right, Justice Strauss," Violet said finally. "We will miss you very much."

"I will miss you, too," she said, and her eyes filled with tears once more. Then they each gave Justice Strauss one last embrace, and followed Mr. and Mrs. Poe to their car. The Baudelaire orphans piled into the backseat, and peered out the back window at Justice Strauss, who was crying and waving to them. Ahead of them were the darkened streets, where Count Olaf had escaped to plan more treachery. Behind them was the kind judge, who had taken such an interest in the three children. To Violet, Klaus, and Sunny, it seemed that Mr. Poe and the law had made the incorrect decision to take them away from the possibility of a happy life with Justice Strauss and toward an unknown fate with some unknown relative. They didn't understand it, but like so many unfortunate events in life, just because you don't understand it doesn't mean it isn't so. The Baudelaires bunched up together against the cold night air, and kept waving out the back window. The car drove farther and farther away, until Justice Strauss was merely a speck in the darkness, and it seemed to the children that they were moving in an aberrant—the word "aberrant" here means "very, very wrong, and causing much grief"—direction.

LEMONY SNICKET was born in a small town where the inhabitants were suspicious and prone to riot. He now lives in the city. During his spare time he gathers evidence and is considered something of an expert by leading authorities.

BRETT HELQUIST was born in Ganado, Arizona, grew up in Orem, Utah, and now lives in New York City. He earned a bachelor's degree in fine arts from Brigham Young University and has been illustrating ever since. His art has appeared in many publications, including *Cricket* magazine and *The New York Times.*

To My Kind Editor,

I am writing to you from the London branch of the Herpetological Society, where I am trying to find out what happened to the reptile collection of Dr. Montgomery Montgomery following the tragic events that occurred while the Baudelaire orphans were in his care.

An associate of mine will place a small waterproof box in the phone booth of the Elektra Hotel at 11 P.M. next Tuesday. Please retrieve it before midnight to avoid it falling into the wrong hands. In the box you will find my description of these terrible events, entitled THE REPTILE ROOM, as well as a map of Lousy Lane, a copy of the film *Zombies in the Snow*, and Dr. Montgomery's recipe for coconut cream cake. I have also managed to track down one of the few photographs of Dr. Lucafont, in order to help Mr. Helquist with his illustrations.

Remember, you are my last hope that the tales of the Baudelaire orphans can finally be told to the general public.

With all due respect,

Lemony Snicket

Lemony Snicket